**Praise f**

"…a book of re-told fairy tales, all in the quirky, matter-of-fact-in-the-face-of-total-nonsense style that I've always loved. They're often dark, sometimes sad, but always endearing, even when they're disturbing."

—Pixelatedgeek.com

**Praise for "The Seventh Bride"**

"…[A] knack for creating colorful, instantly memorable characters, and inhuman creatures capable of inspiring awe and wonder."

—NPR Books

**Praise for "Bryony & Roses"**

"The writing. It is superb. Ursula Vernon/T. Kingfisher, where have you been all my life?"

—The Book Smugglers at Kirkus Reviews

**Praise for "The Raven & The Reindeer"**

"…an exquisitely written retelling of Hans Christian Andersen's The Snow Queen… I love this book with the blazing passion of a thousand suns. I'm sitting here almost crying at the thought that I had to wait until I was fifty-seven (almost fifty-eight!) years old before having a chance to read this book."

—Heather Rose Jones, Daughter of Mystery

***Other Works***

*As T. Kingfisher*

Nine Goblins (Goblinhome Book 1)
Toad Words & Other Stories
The Seventh Bride
Bryony & Roses
Summer in Orcus

*As Ursula Vernon*

From Sofawolf Press:

*Black Dogs* Duology
House of Diamond
Mountain of Iron

*Digger* Series
Digger Omnibus Edition

It Made Sense At The Time

*For kids:*

*Dragonbreath* Series
*Hamster Princess* Series
Castle Hangnail
Nurk: The Strange Surprising Adventures of a Somewhat Brave Shrew

*Anthologies:*

*Comics Squad:* Recess!
Funny Girl
Best of Apex Magazine
The Long List
Peter S. Beagle's *The New Voices of Fantasy*

# Jackalope Wives and Other Stories

by T. Kingfisher

Argyll Productions
Dallas, Texas

Jackalope Wives and Other Stories


This is a work of fiction. Nothing is true, except for the bits that are, and even those don't resemble anybody in particular.


http://www.tkingfisher.com

Published by Argyll Productions
Dallas, Texas
www.argyllproductions.com

ISBN 978-1-61450-403-0

First Edition Trade Paperback September 2017



Typeset in Adobe Garamond Pro and Goudy Old Style.

*For Sigrid*
*who told me to write her a story*

# Table of Contents

# THE KINGFISHER & THE JACKALOPE

It was a few years ago now that I wrote a story for my friend Sigrid, during her stint as editor of Apex Magazine. I had agreed to write one with no idea what I was doing, and so I wrote it at a tattoo parlor, while my husband was getting ink etched into his skin, and that started something happening in my brain about skins, which turned into "Jackalope Wives."

I had never submitted a short story for publication before. I hadn't even thought about it. I hadn't even thought that I was writing short stories, rather than fictional blog post thingies.

"Jackalope Wives" won a Nebula, and at the after-party, I wandered around in a kind of stunned haze. (I had been so confident of *not* winning that my speech had been prepared for the "alternate universe Nebulas" where authors deliver the speech from the alternate universe where they won. It's a grand tradition, and I was excited to deliver my speech from the universe where I had won and also everyone was a giant chicken. I gazed out across a dinner crowd consisting of many of science fiction's greatest luminaries, and heard myself say "Please hold your clucks until the end of the speech…")

At this after-party, an editor from Uncanny Magazine said to me, "We gotta get a story from you!"

I said, "Uh. Okay? I can do that?" while thinking "Wait, really?" and then, much belatedly, "Wait, was that networking? Is networking a thing I just did?"

I am not exactly a marketing genius.

"Jackalope Wives" went on to win a couple more awards and Apex Magazine, perhaps unsurprisingly, wanted another story, which made *two* stories that people wanted and I had somehow agreed to provide. So I wrote two stories, in a bit of a panic, and then I was in a groove and wrote a couple more.

But what did I do with the new ones? I couldn't just bombard these poor people with submissions, could I? That seemed like stalker behavior or at very least entitled—"Hey, you bought a story once, now I will send you ALL OF THEM FOREVER!"—or possibly just sad, like the way that our old Border Collie chased a raccoon up a tree once years ago and always visited that tree first in the yard, forever after, in case the raccoon came back.

And then it occurred to me that I could send a story to a market who hadn't said "Send us a story!" first and maybe they would not send me a pipe bomb by return mail and if they hated it, it wouldn't be weird.

Some of those sold, too. Not all of them, but a couple. My plan seemed to be working—so long as I never submitted anywhere twice, it wouldn't be awkward.

This is not the way to start a short-story career, nor even to blunder into one in midstream. Eventually the editors caught up with me and would start ordering me to send them my *next* story. Or they would pop up with "I really need a novelette for this fundraiser, what have you got?" and then I was Helping Them With A Problem, not Bothering This Busy Person Who Was Nice To Me Once, Probably Out Of Pity.

My cover letters said things like "Here is a thing and I said I'd write you a thing but you don't have to publish it but it's yours if you want it but if not, I'll write you a different one."

I've gotten slightly better at that bit, but not much.

So here is a collection of short stories, which were mostly published elsewhere over the last couple years, but I am putting them all in one place because people asked. I have also included a couple of new ones, because if you're going to lay out money for a collection, you ought get something spiffy and new out of it.

(I am writing this introduction right now in a coffee shop, during a heavy rainstorm, and they are playing Tom Waits. I feel a sort of cheerful, gritty desolation, like smoking the last cigarette at the end of the world. Some of these stories are like that and some of them are funny and some are hard and some are odd, but maybe you'll find something to enjoy.)

Well. Here is a thing, but you don't have to read it, but it's yours if you want to. And if not, I'll write you some different ones.

T. Kingfisher (Ursula Vernon)
Pittsboro
April 2017

# GODMOTHER

*To this day, I still wonder a bit about the bone dog and where it came from. It seems like a book I should write someday.*

You came to me in your cloak made of tatters, with the dog made of bone at your side.

You came to me and demanded to know *why*—why hadn't I been there? Why her, and not you?

What had she done to earn fairy gifts to smooth her way? What did she do to earn the golden dresses and the silver shoes, the care of old women and the kindness of princes?

Why did she get to dance, when *you* had to carve your path of thorns, and bleed for every inch?

I told you that fairy godmothers are a little less than angels. We are given only enough power to hold in our two hands. There is not enough to go around.

I told you that we spend it very grudgingly, and only on those who cannot succeed without our help.

The dancing princess would have died. She would have withered at the first harsh word. She could never have woven the rope from nettles, or built her own dog out of bones.

So I helped her and not you.

I told you that even in the cradle, I knew that you were strong.

You swallowed that, even though the taste was bitter. You were already proud of your strength. (And why wouldn't you be? You have done amazing things. I wish I had the right to be proud of what you've done.)

You walked away, with your tattered cloak swinging, with the bone dog clattering at your side. You walked away, and all you left was the handprint on the doorframe, with your left hand stained with the prince's blood.

I watched you go, and picked the bits of lie out of my teeth with the tip of a worrying tongue.

Truth is, there are too many broken people in the world.

We bet on the ones we think will make it, like birds who feed the strongest chick. We pour love out on those who are already loved and magic on those who only need a little, since a little is all we have to give.

There was nothing much to recommend you as a child. You squalled and whined and cried. You were timid and afraid of strangers.

(And I have to tell you that your breathing was annoying, you made little "uhn! uhn!" noises in your throat at every breath, and certainly this is petty but also it is true.)

Mostly, though, you were easy to forget, so I forgot you.

I did not expect you to survive. You should have died a dozen times and yet you lived, for all you went a darker way.

Well. Good for you. We don't always get it right.

I waited too long to clean the handprint off the doorframe. I left it there for days as a reminder. My eyes dragged over it every time I went out.

I think I hoped that I would learn something.

In the end I washed it off, or tried.

The white paint underneath is stained. In sunlight I hardly notice.

But sometimes now, before I light the candles, I see the shadow of your hand against the door.

# JACKALOPE WIVES

The moon came up and the sun went down. The moonbeams went shattering down to the ground and the jackalope wives took off their skins and danced.

They danced like young deer pawing the ground, they danced like devils let out of hell for the evening. They swung their hips and pranced and drank their fill of cactus-fruit wine.

They were shy creatures, the jackalope wives, though there was nothing shy about the way they danced. You could go your whole life and see no more of them than the flash of a tail vanishing around the backside of a boulder. If you were lucky, you might catch a whole line of them outlined against the sky, on the top of a bluff, the shadow of horns rising off their brows.

And on the half-moon, when new and full were balanced across the saguaro's thorns, they'd come down to the desert and dance.

The young men used to get together and whisper, saying they were gonna catch them a jackalope wife. They'd lay belly down at the edge of the bluff and look down on the fire and the dancing shapes—and they'd go away aching, for all the good it did them.

For the jackalope wives were shy of humans. Their lovers were jackrabbits and antelope bucks, not human men. You couldn't even get too close or they'd take fright and run away. One minute you'd see them kicking their heels up and hear them laugh, then the music would freeze and they'd all look at you with their eyes wide and their ears upswept.

The next second, they'd snatch up their skins and there'd be nothing left but a dozen skinny she-rabbits running off in all directions, and a campfire left that wouldn't burn out 'til morning.

It was uncanny, sure, but they never did anybody any harm. Grandma Harken, who lived down past the well, said that the jackalopes were the daughters of the rain and driving them off would bring on the drought. People said they didn't believe a word of it, but when you live in a desert, you don't take chances.

When the wild music came through town, a couple of notes skittering on the sand, then people knew the jackalope wives were out. They kept the dogs tied up and their brash sons occupied. The town got into the habit of having a dance that night, to keep the boys firmly fixed on human girls and to drown out the notes of the wild music.

Now, it happened there was a young man in town who had a touch of magic on him. It had come down to him on his mother's side, as happens now and again, and it was worse than useless.

A little magic is worse than none, for it draws the wrong sort of attention. It gave this young man feverish eyes and made him sullen. His grandmother used to tell him that it was a miracle he hadn't been drowned as a child, and for her he'd laugh, but not for anyone else.

He was tall and slim and had dark hair and young women found him fascinating.

This sort of thing happens often enough, even with boys as mortal as dirt. There's always one who learned how to brood early and often, and always girls who think they can heal him.

Eventually the girls learn better. Either the hurts are petty little things and they get tired of whining or the hurt's so deep and wide that they drown in it. The smart ones heave themselves back to shore and the slower ones wake up married with a husband who lies around and suffers in their direction. It's part of a dance as old as the jackalopes themselves.

But in this town at this time, the girls hadn't learned and the boy hadn't yet worn out his interest. At the dances, he leaned on the wall with his hands in his pockets and his eyes glittering. Other young men eyed him with dislike. He would slip away early, before the dance was ended, and never marked the eyes that followed him and wished that he would stay.

He himself had one thought and one thought only—to catch a jackalope wife.

They were beautiful creatures, with their long brown legs and their bodies splashed orange by the firelight. They had faces like no mortal woman and they moved like quicksilver and they played music that got down into your bones and thrummed like a sickness.

And there was one—he'd seen her. She danced farther out from the others and her horns were short and sharp as sickles. She was the last one to put on her rabbit skin when the sun came up. Long after the music had stopped, she danced to the rhythm of her own long feet on the sand.

(And now you will ask me about the musicians that played for the jackalope wives. Well, if you can find a place where they've been dancing, you might see something like sidewinder tracks in the dust, and more than that I cannot tell you. The desert chews its secrets right down to the bone.)

So the young man with the touch of magic watched the jackalope wife dancing and you know as well as I do what young men dream about. We will be charitable. She danced a little apart from her fellows, as he walked a little apart from his.

Perhaps he thought she might understand him. Perhaps he found her as interesting as the girls found him.

Perhaps we shouldn't always get what we think we want.

And the jackalope wife danced, out past the circle of the music and the firelight, in the light of the fierce desert stars.

Grandma Harken had settled in for the evening with a shawl on her shoulders and a cat on her lap when somebody started hammering on the door.

"Grandma! Grandma! Come quick—open the door—oh god, Grandma, you have to help me—"

She knew that voice just fine. It was her own grandson, her daughter Eva's boy. Pretty and useless and charming when he set out to be.

She dumped the cat off her lap and stomped to the door. What trouble had the young fool gotten himself into?

"Sweet Saint Anthony," she muttered, "let him not have gotten some fool girl in a family way. That's just what we need."

She flung the door open and there was Eva's son and there was a girl and for a moment her worst fears were realized.

Then she saw what was huddled in the circle of her grandson's arms, and her worst fears were stomped flat and replaced by far greater ones.

"Oh Mary," she said. "Oh, Jesus, Mary and Joseph. Oh blessed Saint Anthony, you've caught a jackalope wife."

Her first impulse was to slam the door and lock the sight away.

Her grandson caught the edge of the door and hauled it open. His knuckles were raw and blistered. "Let me in," he said. He'd been crying and there was dust on his face, stuck to the tracks of tears. "Let me in, let me in, oh god, Grandma, you have to help me, it's all gone wrong—"

Grandma took two steps back, while he half-dragged the jackalope into the house. He dropped her down in front of the hearth and grabbed for his grandmother's hands. "Grandma—"

She ignored him and dropped to her knees. The thing across her hearth was hardly human. "What have you done?" she said. "What did you do to her?"

"Nothing!" he said, recoiling.

"Don't look at that and tell me 'Nothing!' What in the name of our lord did you do to that girl?"

He stared down at his blistered hands. "Her skin," he mumbled. "The rabbit skin. You know."

"I do indeed," she said grimly. "Oh yes, I do. What did you do, you damned young fool? Caught up her skin and hid it from her to keep her changing?"

The jackalope wife stirred on the hearth and made a sound between a whimper and a sob.

"She was waiting for me!" he said. "She knew I was there! I'd been—we'd—I watched her, and she knew I was out there, and she let me get up close—I thought we could talk—"

Grandma Harken clenched one hand into a fist and rested her forehead on it.

"I grabbed the skin—I mean—it was right there—she was watching—I thought she *wanted* me to have it—"

She turned and looked at him. He sank down in her chair, all his grace gone.

"You have to burn it," mumbled her grandson. He slid down a little further in her chair. "You're supposed to burn it. Everybody knows. To keep them changing."

"Yes," said Grandma Harken, curling her lip. "Yes, that's the way of it, right enough." She took the jackalope wife's shoulders and turned her toward the lamp light.

She was a horror. Her hands were human enough, but she had a jackrabbit's feet and a jackrabbit's eyes. They were set too wide apart in a human face, with a cleft lip and long rabbit ears. Her horns were short, sharp spikes on her brow.

The jackalope wife let out another sob and tried to curl back into a ball. There were burnt patches on her arms and legs, a long red weal down her face. The fur across her breasts and belly was singed. She stank of urine and burning hair.

*"What did you do?"*

"I threw it in the fire," he said. "You're supposed to. But she screamed—she wasn't supposed to scream—nobody said they screamed—and I thought she was dying, and I didn't want to *hurt* her—I pulled it back out—"

He looked up at her with his feverish eyes, that useless, beautiful boy, and said "I didn't *want* to hurt her. I thought I was supposed to—I gave her the skin back, she put it on, but then she fell down—it wasn't supposed to work like that!"

Grandma Harken sat back. She exhaled very slowly. She was calm. She was going to be calm, because otherwise she was going to pick up the fire poker and club her own flesh and blood over the head with it.

*And even that might not knock some sense into him. Oh, Eva, Eva, my dear, what a useless son you've raised. Who would have thought he had so much ambition in him, to catch a jackalope wife?*

"You goddamn stupid fool," she said. Every word slammed like a shutter in the wind. "Oh, you goddamn stupid fool. If you're going to catch a jackalope wife, you burn the hide down to ashes and never mind how she screams."

"But it sounded like it was hurting her!" he shot back. "You weren't there! She screamed like a dying rabbit!"

"Of course it hurts her!" yelled Grandma. "You think you can have your skin and your freedom burned away in front of you and not scream? Sweet mother Mary, boy, think about what you're doing! Be cruel or be kind, but don't be both, because now you've made a mess you can't clean up in a hurry."

She stood up, breathing hard, and looked down at the wreck on her hearth. She could see it now, as clear as if she'd been standing there. The fool boy had been so shocked he'd yanked the burning skin back out. And the jackalope wife had one thought only and pulled on the burning hide—

Oh yes, she could see it clear.

Half gone, at least, if she was any judge. There couldn't have been more than few scraps of fur left unburnt. He'd waited through at least one scream—or no, that was unkind.

More likely he'd dithered and looked for a stick and didn't want to grab for it with his bare hands. Though by the look of his hands, he'd done just that in the end.

And the others were long gone by then and couldn't stop her. There ought to have been one, at least, smart enough to know that you didn't put on a half-burnt rabbit skin.

"Why does she look like that?" whispered her grandson, huddled into his chair.

"Because she's trapped betwixt and between. You did that, with your goddamn pity. You should have let it burn. Or better yet, left her alone and never gone out in the desert at all."

"She was beautiful," he said. As if it were a reason.

As if it mattered.

As if it had ever mattered.

"Get out," said Grandma wearily. "Tell your mother to make up a poultice for your hands. You did right at the end, bringing her here, even if you made a mess of the rest, from first to last."

He scrambled to his feet and ran for the door.

On the threshold, he paused, and looked back. "You—you can fix her, right?"

Grandma let out a high bark, like a bitch-fox, barely a laugh at all. "No. No one can fix this, you stupid boy. This is broken past mending. All I can do is pick up the pieces."

He ran. The door slammed shut, and left her alone with the wreckage of the jackalope wife.

She treated the burns and they healed. But there was nothing to be done for the shape of the jackalope's face, or the too-wide eyes, or the horns shaped like a sickle moon.

At first, Grandma worried that the townspeople would see her, and lord knew what would happen then. But the jackalope wife was the color of dust and she still had a wild animal's stillness. When somebody called, she lay flat in the garden, down among the beans, and nobody saw her at all.

The only person she didn't hide from was Eva, Grandma's daughter. There was no chance that she mistook them for each other—Eva was round and plump and comfortable, the way Grandma's second husband, Eva's father, had been round and plump and comfortable.

*Maybe we smell alike,* thought Grandma. *It would make sense, I suppose.*

Eva's son didn't come around at all.

"He thinks you're mad at him," said Eva mildly.

"He thinks correctly," said Grandma.

She and Eva sat on the porch together, shelling beans, while the jackalope wife limped around the garden. The hairless places weren't so obvious now, and the faint stripes across her legs might have been dust. If you didn't look directly at her, she might almost have been human.

"She's gotten good with the crutch," said Eva. "I suppose she can't walk?"

"Not well," said Grandma. "Her feet weren't made to stand up like that. She can do it, but it's a terrible strain."

"And talk?"

"No," said Grandma shortly. The jackalope wife had tried, once, and the noises she'd made were so terrible that it had reduced them both to weeping. She hadn't tried again. "She understands well enough, I suppose."

The jackalope wife sat down, slowly, in the shadow of the scarlet runner beans. A hummingbird zipped inches from her head, dabbing its bill into the flowers, and the jackalope's face turned, unsmiling, to follow it.

"He's not a bad boy, you know," said Eva, not looking at her mother. "He didn't mean to do her harm."

Grandma let out an explosive snort. "Jesus, Mary and Joseph! It doesn't matter what he *meant* to do. He should have left well enough alone, and if he couldn't do that, he should have finished what he started." She scowled down at the beans. They were striped red and white and the pods came apart easily in her gnarled hands. "Better all the way human than this. Better he'd bashed her head in with a rock than *this.*"

"Better for her, or better for you?" asked Eva, who was only a fool about her son and knew her mother well.

Grandma snorted again. The hummingbird buzzed away. The jackalope wife lay still in the shadows, with only her thin ribs going up and down.

"You could have finished it, too," said Eva softly. "I've seen you kill chickens. She'd probably lay her head on the chopping block if you asked."

"She probably would," said Grandma. She looked away from Eva's weak, wise eyes. "But I'm a damn fool as well."

Her daughter smiled. "Maybe it runs in families."

Grandma Harken got up before dawn the next morning and went rummaging around the house.

"Well," she said. She pulled a dead mouse out of a mousetrap and took a half-dozen cigarettes down from behind the clock. She filled three water bottles and strapped them around her waist. "Well. I suppose we've done as much as humans can do, and now it's up to somebody else."

She went out into the garden and found the jackalope wife asleep under the stairs. "Come on," she said. "Wake up."

The air was cool and gray. The jackalope wife looked at her with doe-dark eyes and didn't move, and if she were a human, Grandma Harken would have itched to slap her.

*Pay attention! Get mad! Do something!*

But she wasn't human and rabbits freeze when they're scared past running. So Grandma gritted her teeth and reached down a hand and pulled the jackalope wife up into the pre-dawn dark.

They moved slow, the two of them. Grandma was old and carrying water for two, and the girl was on a crutch. The sun came up and the cicadas burnt the air with their wings.

A coyote watched them from up on the hillside. The jackalope wife looked up at him, recoiled, and Grandma laid a hand on her arm.

"Don't worry," she said. "I ain't got the patience for coyotes. They'd maybe fix you up but we'd both be stuck in a tale past telling, and I'm too old for that. Come on."

They went a little further on, past a wash and a watering hole. There were palo verde trees spreading thin green shade over the water. A javelina looked up at them from the edge and stamped her hooved feet. Her children scraped their tusks together and grunted.

Grandma slid and slithered down the slope to the far side of the water and refilled the water bottles. "Not them either," she said to the jackalope wife. "They'll talk the legs off a wooden sheep. We'd both be dead of old age before they'd figured out what time to start."

The javelina dropped their heads and ignored them as they left the wash behind.

The sun was overhead and the sky turned turquoise, a color so hard you could bash your knuckles on it. A raven croaked overhead and another one snickered somewhere off to the east.

The jackalope wife paused, leaning on her crutch, and looked up at the wings with longing.

"Oh no," said Grandma. "I've got no patience for riddle games, and in the end they always eat someone's eyes. Relax, child. We're nearly there."

The last stretch was cruelly hard, up the side of a bluff. The sand was soft underfoot and miserably hard for a girl walking with a crutch. Grandma had to half-carry the jackalope wife at the end. She weighed no more than a child, but children are heavy and it took them both a long time.

At the top was a high fractured stone that cast a finger of shadow like the wedge of a sundial. Sand and sky and shadow and stone. Grandma Harken nodded, content.

"It'll do," she said. "It'll do." She laid the jackalope wife down in the shadow and laid her tools out on the stone. Cigarettes and dead mouse and a scrap of burnt fur from the jackalope's breast. "It'll do."

Then she sat down in the shadow herself and arranged her skirts.

She waited.

The sun went overhead and the level in the water bottle went down. The sun started to sink and the wind hissed and the jackalope wife was asleep or dead.

The ravens croaked a conversation to each other, from the branches of a palo verde tree, and whatever one said made the other one laugh.

"Well," said a voice behind Grandma's right ear, "lookee what we have here."

"Jesus, Mary and Joseph!"

"Don't see them out here often," he said. "Not the right sort of place." He considered. "Your Saint Anthony, now…him I think I've seen. He understood about deserts."

Grandma's lips twisted. "Father of Rabbits," she said sourly. "Wasn't trying to call you up."

"Oh, I know." The Father of Rabbits grinned. "But you know I've always had a soft spot for you, Maggie Harken."

He sat down beside her on his heels. He looked like an old Mexican man, wearing a button-down shirt without any buttons. His hair was silver gray as a rabbit's fur. Grandma wasn't fooled for a minute.

"Get lonely down there in your town, Maggie?" he asked. "Did you come out here for a little wild company?"

Grandma Harken leaned over to the jackalope wife and smoothed one long ear back from her face. She looked up at them both with wide, uncomprehending eyes.

"Shit," said the Father of Rabbits. "Never seen that before." He lit a cigarette and blew the smoke into the air. "What did you do to her, Maggie?"

"I didn't do a damn thing, except not let her die when I should have."

"There's those would say that was more than enough." He exhaled another lungful of smoke.

"She put on a half-burnt skin. Don't suppose you can fix her up?" It cost Grandma a lot of pride to say that, and the Father of Rabbits tipped his chin in acknowledgment.

"Ha! No. If it was loose I could fix it up, maybe, but I couldn't get it off her now with a knife." He took another drag on the cigarette. "Now I see why you wanted one of the Patterned People."

Grandma nodded stiffly.

The Father of Rabbits shook his head. "He might want a life, you know. Piddly little dead mouse might not be enough."

"Then he can have mine."

"Ah, Maggie, Maggie...You'd have made a fine rabbit, once. Too many stones in your belly now." He shook his head regretfully. "Besides, it's not *your* life he's owed."

"It's my life he'd be getting. My kin did it, it's up to me to put it right." It occurred to her that she should have left Eva a note, telling her to send the fool boy back East, away from the desert.

Well. Too late now. Either she'd raised a fool for a daughter or not, and likely she wouldn't be around to tell.

"Suppose we'll find out," said the Father of Rabbits, and nodded.

A man came around the edge of the standing stone. He moved quick then slow and his eyes didn't blink. He was naked and his skin was covered in painted diamonds.

Grandma Harken bowed to him, because the Patterned People can't hear speech.

He looked at her and the Father of Rabbits and the jackalope wife. He looked down at the stone in front of him.

The cigarettes he ignored. The mouse he scooped up in two fingers and dropped into his mouth.

Then he crouched there, for a long time. He was so still that it made Grandma's eyes water, and she had to look away.

"Suppose he does it," said the Father of Rabbits. "Suppose he sheds that skin right off her. Then what? You've got a human left over, not a jackalope wife."

Grandma stared down at her bony hands. "It's not so bad, being a human," she said. "You make do. And it's got to be better than that."

She jerked her chin in the direction of the jackalope wife.

"Still meddling, Maggie?" said the Father of Rabbits.

"And what do you call what you're doing?"

He grinned.

The Patterned Man stood up and nodded to the jackalope wife.

She looked at Grandma, who met her too-wide eyes. "He'll kill you," the old woman said. "Or cure you. Or maybe both. You don't have to do it. This is the bit where you get a choice. But when it's over, you'll be all the way something, even if it's just all the way dead."

The jackalope wife nodded.

She left the crutch lying on the stones and stood up. Rabbit legs weren't meant for it, but she walked three steps and the Patterned Man opened his arms and caught her.

He bit her on the forearm, where the thick veins run, and sank his teeth in up to the gums. Grandma cursed.

"Easy now," said the Father of Rabbits, putting a hand on her shoulder. "He's one of the Patterned People, and they only know the one way."

The jackalope wife's eyes rolled back in her head, and she sagged down onto the stone.

He set her down gently and picked up one of the cigarettes.

Grandma Harken stepped forward. She rolled both her sleeves up to the elbow and offered him her wrists.

The Patterned Man stared at her, unblinking. The ravens laughed to themselves at the bottom of the wash. Then he dipped his head and bowed to Grandma Harken and a rattlesnake as long as a man slithered away into the evening.

She let out a breath she didn't know she'd been holding. "He didn't ask for a life."

The Father of Rabbits grinned. "Ah, you know. Maybe he wasn't hungry. Maybe it was enough you made the offer."

"Maybe I'm too old and stringy," she said.

"Could be that, too."

The jackalope wife was breathing. Her pulse went fast then slow. Grandma sat down beside her and held her wrist between her own callused palms.

"How long you going to wait?" asked the Father of Rabbits.

"As long as it takes," she snapped back.

The sun went down while they were waiting. The coyotes sang up the moon. It was half-full, half-new, halfway between one thing and the other.

"She doesn't have to stay human, you know," said the Father of Rabbits. He picked up the cigarettes that the Patterned Man had left behind and offered one to Grandma.

"She doesn't have a jackalope skin any more."

He grinned. She could just see his teeth flash white in the dark. "Give her yours."

"I burned it," said Grandma Harken, sitting up ramrod straight. "I found where he hid it after he died and I burned it myself. Because I had a new husband and a little bitty baby girl and all I could think about was leaving them both behind and go dance."

The Father of Rabbits exhaled slowly in the dark.

"It was easier that way," she said. "You get over what you *can't* have faster that you get over what you *could.* And we shouldn't always get what we think we want."

They sat in silence at the top of the bluff. Between Grandma's hands, the pulse beat steady and strong.

"I never did like your first husband much," said the Father of Rabbits.

"Well," she said. She lit her cigarette off his. "He taught me how to swear. And the second one was better."

The jackalope wife stirred and stretched. Something flaked off her in long strands, like burnt scraps of paper, like a snake's skin shedding away. The wind tugged at them and sent them spinning off the side of the bluff.

From down in the desert, they heard the first notes of a sudden wild music.

"It happens I might have a spare skin," said the Father of Rabbits. He reached into his pack and pulled out a long gray roll of rabbit skin. The jackalope wife's eyes went wide and her body shook with longing, but it was human longing and a human body shaking.

"Where'd you get that?" asked Grandma Harken, suspicious.

"Oh, well, you know." He waved a hand. "Pulled it out of a fire once—must have been forty years ago now. Took some doing to fix it up again, but some people owed me favors. Suppose she might as well have it...Unless you want it?"

He held it out to Grandma Harken.

She took it in her hands and stroked it. It was as soft as it had been fifty years ago. The small sickle horns were hard weights in her hands.

"You were a hell of a dancer," said the Father of Rabbits.

"Still am," said Grandma Harken, and she flung the jackalope skin over the shoulders of the human jackalope wife.

It went on like it had been made for her, like it was her own. There was a jagged scar down one foreleg where the rattlesnake had bit her. She leapt up and darted away, circled back once and bumped Grandma's hand with her nose—and then she was bounding down the path from the top of the bluff.

The Father of Rabbits let out a long sigh. "Still are," he agreed.

"It's different when you got a choice," said Grandma Harken.

They shared another cigarette under the standing stone.

Down in the desert, the music played and the jackalope wives danced. And one scarred jackalope went leaping into the circle of firelight and danced like a demon, while the moon laid down across the saguaro's thorns.

# WOODEN FEATHERS

*This is the story that the editor from Uncanny Magazine got. It came to me one morning and I had to write it right that minute, which, since it turned out to be about seven thousand words, left me with my brain feeling like a wrung-out sponge. Occasionally it happens like that. It's a great time saver, but it does take bit of a physical toll.*

The carving was going badly.

Sarah examined the duck decoy before her and sighed. The bill was shaped entirely wrong. It was supposed to be a mallard, but she hadn't taken enough off before she began shaping and now the bill was half again as long as it should be.

*I'll flare the bill and make it a Northern Shoveler*, she decided. *Nobody has to know that it was supposed to be a mallard.*

Two customers came in, so she set down the knife and put on her best customer service expression. "Hi, there!"

Two middle-aged women nodded to her. They gave the stall a professional once-over, looking for bargains or hidden treasure, then left again without speaking.

*Give it up, ladies. The internet got rid of all that. Go bid on storage units or estate trunks or something if you're hoping to strike it big.*

Well, you didn't say things like that aloud. Not to the customers, anyway. Sarah picked up the knife and turned the decoy around. The hind ends of many ducks looked alike. She wouldn't have to change anything much to transform her mallard.

Rauf, who ran the stall across the way, waved to her. She liked Rauf. He sold popcorn and boiled peanuts and curry rub and never complained about sawdust getting tracked across the floor.

The sawdust got everywhere, but people liked to watch a carver work. On a good day they would come in and stare for long enough that they felt guilty and bought something small. She did a pretty good business in tiny duck keychains that way.

Given that there were three other woodworkers in the flea market, all of them better than she was, Sarah figured that she needed all the help she could get.

She didn't talk to the other carvers much. The old-timers at the market wouldn't talk to you until you'd been there at least a couple of years.

Another customer came in. She looked up and stifled a sigh.

"Hey, there," she said. "Good to see you again."

The old man nodded.

He was a repeat customer, but she'd never learned his name. He wore a dusty black suit with frayed bits at the cuffs. The only things that moved quickly about him were his hands. When he picked up one of her carvings, his face stayed old but his hands became young, gnarled but deft. He ran his thumbs over the carved edges of the feathers, traced a circle around the glass eye, and looked up at her inquiringly.

"Common Goldeneye," she said. Which was true enough, and nobody needed to know that it had started life as a Long-Tailed Duck, but she'd knocked the tail off and then had to get creative.

He nodded. He set the duck down and his hands were old again. He slowly opened his wallet and began to pull out wrinkled bills. The wallet was even more frayed than the suit.

Sarah took the money. She could smell him on it—old man smell, Bengay and fabric washed so many times that it had lost any hope of getting clean.

He came in every week and bought the cheapest of her decoys. He paid cash and brought his own shopping bag over his arm. Sarah worried about him.

"There's a fifteen percent discount," she said, sliding the change back.

"There is?" His voice was so quiet she had to strain to hear it over the sounds of the market.

"Yeah," said Sarah, who had just made it up on the spot. "To celebrate—um—the new duck stamp coming out." She waved her hand toward the wall, where she'd put up a poster just this morning. "It's a Ruddy Duck."

"Is it?" He looked at the poster thoughtfully. She sometimes thought, for a man who bought so many decoys, that he knew very little about ducks.

He took the change and put it very slowly away, then slipped the decoy into his bag. She had stopped offering to wrap them months ago. Then he made his slow way out of the stall and vanished into the crowd.

She slumped back on her stool. She needed the money, but she felt strange taking it from the old man. Why would anyone buy a carved duck decoy every single week?

On good days, she pretended that he was secretly a millionaire, one of the ones who lived cheap, but that he was overcome by admiration for her duck carvings and had to own them.

On most days, she figured that he had a shopping addiction.

Rauf came over, holding a bag of popcorn. "Here," he said. "We're about to start a new batch and you haven't eaten all morning."

"Thanks, Rauf." She wiped her hands off and took a handful. "How's it going?"

"Slow." He shrugged. "August is always bad. Everybody's spent all their vacation money and now they're looking at back to school sales."

Sarah nodded. Hand-carved ducks sold much worse than popcorn.

"I see old Jep came by."

"Who?"

"Jep. Just now." Rauf waved toward the gap in her line of carvings. "Comes in every week, doesn't he?"

"Oh, him! Yeah. Didn't know he had a name." *Jep*. It seemed like a name for a mountain moonshiner, not an old, frayed man. Then again, maybe he'd been a moonshiner in his youth, who knew?

"He used to be a carver," said Rauf, promptly dashing the moonshiner fantasy. "Had a stall over on the high-rent side. That was years ago, though."

"He was?" Sarah blinked.

"Oh, yeah." Rauf grinned. "He did a big carousel over in Nag's Head. Had photos up in his stall. Horses and dolphins and seagulls big enough to ride."

Sarah stared down into the bag of popcorn, wondering how she should feel about that.

"You said he *used* to be a carver..." she said.

"He stopped after his wife got sick," said Rauf, the grin fading. "Closed up his stall. They sell custom hammocks or something in it now. I don't know if he's done anything since."

"He must've," said Sarah. She could not imagine not carving. Even when business was dreadful and she had to spend half the income from waitressing just to keep the stall open, it never occurred to her to quit.

She wouldn't have lasted three days. She'd be sitting on the couch and her hands would start to itch for sandpaper and a knife. She'd end up carving the arm of the couch if she couldn't get a wooden blank.

Rauf shrugged. "I don't know. You could ask him."

Sarah turned the regrettable mallard-turned-shoveler around. "Maybe I will."

But when he came in the next week, she asked him a different question instead.

"Did you make these?"

Jep looked up at her. No emotion crossed the long, dragged lines of his face, but she thought that she'd surprised him.

She held out her phone, with the pictures of the carousel in Nag's Head on it.

He did not take it, but he bent down to look at the screen. After a moment he said "Yes. Those were mine."

He did not look like a man who was proud. He looked like a soldier admitting that he had been to war. He bought the cheapest decoy, put it into his bag, and shuffled out of the shop.

Sarah stared after him, and then down at the photos of the carousel.

Many carousels were works of art. This was more. This was—she didn't have the words—*glory.*

The horses were a riot of color, gilded and painted, their heads thrown back or bowed far forward under scarlet reins. Smiling dolphins leapt and cavorted between the horses. There was a gull with its beak open, laughing, and a narwhal with a golden horn and a pelican so large that a child could ride in the pouch.

Sarah's favorite was a walrus. It was snow white, with a blue saddle, and its tusks were scrimshawed with starfish and ships. Its lumpy, bristly face was screwed up in a grin of delight. In the photo, a little girl had her arms as far around it as they could go, and she was grinning too.

*A carousel like that must have cost a million dollars,* she thought. *He must have charged tons for it. I hope he's rich. I hope.*

She knew all too well how much artists undercut themselves. She was painting the shoveler this week, and if she made thirty dollars worth of profit on the accursed thing, she'd be happy.

The next week, when Jep came in, she asked him if he was still carving.

He shook his head, mutely. He bought the shoveler and went away again.

Sarah was beginning to feel as if she had struck some kind of fairy-tale bargain. One carving bought one question, no more.

The shoveler had barely been worth a headshake anyway. She sighed.

Her current project was a Ruddy Duck, like the one of the stamp. They were small, cheerful ducks, with jaunty tails. They also had a specific enough shape that she wasn't going to be able to turn it into anything else if she screwed up.

When Jep came in this time, she paused before she took his money, and said "Why do you keep buying my carvings?"

He stared down at the floor.

The silence went on so long that she took his money and passed him his change, afraid that she had offended him somehow.

*No—surely I didn't. "Why are you buying this?" isn't a weird question for an artist to ask!*

Jep's lips moved. She had to strain to hear him over the sound of Rauf's popcorn maker.

He said "They're the cheapest ones at the flea market."

He looked up, once, before he left the stall. She hoped that his eyes were as old as the rest of him, because she knew how stricken she must look. Her face felt hot.

She went to the bathroom, full of shoppers complaining to each other about the price of discount socks and how crowded everything was, and splashed water on her face. She was not going to cry in front of the customers.

*Well. What did you expect him to say? That he could see your potential? That those crappy ducks were signs of genius? That he wanted to collect them before you got famous and they sold for thousands of bucks apiece?*

She wiped her face with a paper towel. Yes. She had wanted him to say those things. She had wanted to think that the man who had carved those carousel beasts had found something good in her work.

*At least it's better than "because I'm passionately in love with you."*

She choked back a laugh at that, or maybe it was a sob. One of the shoppers looked at her curiously, but didn't ask.

She closed up shop early that day, told Rauf she had a headache, and went home.

When the next weekend rolled around, Sarah wondered if he'd even come back. He had to know he'd upset her.

*Unless something's gone wrong. Maybe he's got dementia or something. Maybe he keeps buying ducks because he can't help it.*

She wondered what his house looked like. There had to be dozens of decoys by now. She pictured ducks on every available surface, rooms full of jumbled carvings.

Maybe she should stop selling them to him.

She wondered if that would stop him, or if he would just go to the next cheapest person in line.

He came in, and her stomach dropped.

*Be professional. You're a pro. Smile and nod. It doesn't matter why he buys it, only that you can pay the rent on the stall.*

He picked up the smallest carving. It was an older one, a mallard, and she had finally accepted that it was never going to sell and had dropped the price on it.

Her good intentions deserted her.

"It's not very good," she said.

He shook his head. The loose skin under his throat moved. "No," he said. "It isn't."

Sarah let out a single, frustrated sob. "Then why are you buying it? And what am I doing *wrong?*"

She put her face in her hands.

She heard Jep shift from foot to foot, and then he made his slow way up to the counter, and around it. He put one hand on her shoulder and squeezed, harder and heavier than she would have expected.

"You're cutting too slow," he said.

She wiped her eyes on the back of her wrist. "W-what?"

He touched the half-carved ruddy, where it sat clamped in the vise. "You're working too slow," he said. He pointed to a wobbling line across a feather. "It slips and gouges here. You're afraid to go faster, so the cuts aren't clean."

He took the carving knife from the bench and made a single unhurried cut, still faster than anything she had ever done. A curl of wood came up behind it, and then it was the edge of the duck's wing, tucked against its body, and the line was long and clean and perfect.

"I can't do that!" said Sarah. And then, so fast that she almost tripped over her own words, *"Thank you."*

Jep looked at her. His immobile face cracked a little, and he said "Will you drive me home? I want to show you something."

It was madness driving a strange man home, but she did it anyway. She had her cell phone and Rauf knew what was happening and anyway, Jep was so old that if he tried to kill her, he'd probably have a heart attack stabbing her. She opened the door of her battered truck and let him climb into the cab.

He lived only a few blocks from the flea market, down a shaded street. The lawns were by turns overgrown and painfully, shabbily tidy.

Jep's house was one of the tidy ones. He led her down the walk and paused in front of the battered wrought iron down.

"Please don't tell anyone about this," he said. "It's not…it's nothing…"

He stopped, as if he had run out of words. Sarah said, "I won't," and hoped again that she wasn't making a very stupid mistake.

He unlocked the door. Inside, it was very dim and she could hear a TV blaring somewhere in another room. The linoleum was a dreadful pattern from the Seventies and there was a little plaster crucifix on one wall, and a painting of sheep on the other. The sheep were fluffy and big-eyed and Sarah couldn't imagine Jep buying such a thing.

He led her past the kitchen, to the back of the house and a short hallway and a plain wooden door. She could hear the TV through it. He unlocked that, too, and stepped through the doorway in front of her. She caught a glimpse of a room with a couch and a TV and debris littering the floor.

"Hello, old man," said a creaking, clacking voice. "Come to feed me?"

Sarah's first thought was that the light from the TV was casting some awful shadow on the person sitting on the couch.

Her second was that she wanted out of the house, and she wanted out of it now, and she would have run if she thought her legs could carry her.

There was a marionette on the couch.

It was the size of a human-being. It had a mouth like a nutcracker and its face was carved like a Roman god. Curls of gilded hair ringed its head.

*Someone is working it—someone—there's a puppeteer up on the ceiling or something—*

It turned its head at her, and she saw its expression change. The wood moved.

She backed up so fast that her spine struck the wall opposite. She slid down it. She thought she might be sick.

*It can't be real wood. It's a person painted to look like a marionette. It's a mask or a special effect or* something.

It snickered. "I can't eat *her*," said the marionette. It clacked its hollow jaws at her. "Or I could try, but neither of us will enjoy it."

"That's enough," said Jep.

The TV was showing some ridiculous daytime game show. The host gestured for an audience member to come down and try their luck.

*Are you the lucky person who's seen a horror and is going to walk away alive? Come on down!*

"Enough," said the marionette. Its voice was nothing like human. "Never enough. Hasn't been enough since the old lady died."

Jep reached in his bag and took out the carved mallard. He threw it toward the couch.

The marionette caught it neatly out of midair—*it can't be on strings, no puppeteer on earth could make a thing on strings do that*—and grabbed the decoy's neck. She could see the fingers, beautifully articulated, each ball joint perfect, ending in tapered points.

The duck carving came alive.

Sarah watched as her poor mangled mallard suddenly stretched out its wings. She caught a glimpse of carved wooden feathers, the bill opening, the legs—she hadn't even carved legs! Where had they come from?—flailing.

It hung poised for a moment, as if in flight, and then the marionette wrung its neck.

The decoy collapsed. It was still wood, it could only be wood, but it was wood carved like a dead bird, the wings trailing down.

The marionette opened its mouth impossibly wide, showing a black, toothless opening that ran halfway down the thing's throat, and bit into the mallard's breast.

Wood splintered. The marionette chewed. Sawdust fell down around it, and a single wooden feather drifted to the floor.

It took another bite, and another, then wiped its mouth.

"Where's my horse, old man?" asked the marionette.

The game show host on TV showed the contestants what they could win. Door after door opened, revealing new cars and shiny appliances, and the marionette turned away. It lowered its gaping mouth to the body of the duck and chewed as it watched.

Jep came out and closed the door. He locked it again, his movements as slow as when he came into the stall.

"What," said Sarah from the floor. "What. What?" She looked up at him, half in fear, half hoping that he would confirm what she thought she'd seen. "What was that? What—who—"

He helped her into the kitchen and then he made tea. When he opened the pantry to get the tea bags, she could see empty shelves, a few cans, and a pink hat on a hook that certainly wasn't his.

She could hear the TV from down the hall still, and knowing what was sitting there and watching the screen made her shudder.

If she thought too closely, she'd go completely mad. Perhaps she'd gone mad already.

*Did my mallard really come alive? Did it really—no, it couldn't have—it was some kind of trick, he had a live duck in his bag all this time—*

Which was completely ridiculous. He'd had the bag on his lap in the truck. She would have noticed if he was carrying a live duck around in it.

She started to laugh and stuffed both hands in her mouth to stop it.

"He can only eat wooden meat," said Jep. He pushed the mug of tea in front of her. It had a faded picture of a kitten on it. The ancient avocado refrigerator hummed soothingly. "He doesn't eat much of it, not really. A duck will last him all week. And the wood doesn't go bad."

Sarah stared across the table at him. She wondered if he'd let her go, if she ran.

"He's wood," she said.

Jep nodded.

"He's alive, though."

Jep nodded again.

Sarah held the mug of tea and her hands shook so badly that she had to set it back down on the table. The faded kitten ogled at her.

"My wife wanted a son," he said. "We couldn't have one. So I carved him." He looked into his own tea. "It's not a good idea to do that."

"No," said Sarah in a high voice. "No, I bet it isn't!"

It was impossible, of course. She knew that it was impossible.

She thought of the carved walrus and the laughing gull and the prancing horses.

If any man on earth could have brought a carving to life, it would have been the person who carved those horses.

"How did you do it?" she whispered.

Jep shrugged. "Wood's half alive already," he said. "You know. A good carving's not a dead thing, if you put enough of your heart into it."

Sarah clutched the mug of tea. It was hot enough that her hands were starting to burn, but she had to hold onto something.

Yes. She did know. But there was a great deal of distance between believing that good art had a life of its own, and having a thing that sat in a room and tore apart carved birds with its clacking mouth.

"I think more people can do it than let on," said Jep. "But you shouldn't make people. It's not good, making people like that."

"You've been feeding him my carvings," said Sarah. She said it out loud and felt nothing at all. She knew that she should feel something—grief, perhaps, or outrage. They had not been very good carvings, but she had worked hard on them. She didn't expect them to end up in museums, but she'd thought that maybe someone was appreciating them.

Apparently they had been appreciated briefly, and only once.

She thought of the mallard coming to life and had to put the tea down and put her hands over her mouth.

Had all her poor carvings come to life at the last? Had they been alive just so that they could die?

Now she felt something, but it was so huge and terrible that she didn't dare let it out.

"I'm sorry," said Jep. "They have to be hand-carved. I tried the mass-produced ones and they don't come alive. He can't eat them."

He reached across the table and touched her hand, tentatively. "It's not that yours are bad. It's just…I'm on a fixed income. I can't afford anyone else's."

She took a burning gulp of tea. It seared all the way down.

When she could speak again, she said "Why don't you carve them yourself?"

He rose from the table and led her to the back door.

There were two sets of boots by it. One was large and black and looked like the footwear equivalent of Jep's suit.

The other pair were smaller and faded and had pink flowers on them. She looked away.

It was entirely possible, of course, that Jep planned to kill her, now that she knew his terrible secret, and bury her in the backyard. But stepping outside was a relief and it was hard to believe, as the sunlight fell over her, what lay in the house behind her.

There was a little wooden shed behind the house. He led her to it and opened the door.

It was almost completely empty. There was a table in one corner, and few pieces of wood slid through the rafters. Jars of nails caught the light from the windowsill.

It smelled of pine and dust. Sarah turned her head, tracing pale squares on the floor, where machinery had been and now was gone. There were not even spiderwebs in the corners.

*So poor they can't afford cobwebs*, her mother had said once, about a relative. And here it was. The only things left were the shop lights overhead, their bulbs gone dim, but still she recognized it.

"This was your woodshop, wasn't it?" said Sarah.

Jep nodded. There was no emotion on his face, not even grief. "When my wife was sick, I had to sell the tools. We couldn't afford the meds otherwise. We would have lost the house, and then someone would have found him."

He straightened. "I didn't tell her, of course. I said I'd got a commission. She never knew."

There was a note in his voice that at first she thought was bitterness, and then recognized.

Pride.

*He sold all his equipment to pay for his wife's care. And he's proud that she never found out about it.*

She had the sensation again of standing on the edge of an emotion so huge that if she let it reach her, she would drown.

"This is the only thing left," Jep said. He pointed behind her, up against the wall, and she turned. "Couldn't find a buyer, since it wasn't done."

It was a horse.

It stood twice the size of the carousel horses, the neck arched. Its face was exquisitely carved, its front hooves feathered like a draft horse. The mane rippled. There was no bridle, no saddle, hardly any decoration. It needed none.

The back half, though, was barely roughed in. The hooves were square and the tail was a crude rectangle of wood. She could see the exact point where he had set down the chisel, the different coloration of the wood.

*He was working on this when his wife got sick.*

It was a crime that it had never been finished.

*And what do you want him to finish it with? His teeth?*

She thought of the marionette saying *Where's my horse, old man?*

She stepped out of the shed and went around the house, toward her truck. Astonishingly, she did not seem to be dead. Jep walked with her, and didn't show any sign of stopping her.

"Don't think too badly of him," he said. "My wife tried to teach him some manners. She loved him. He misses her."

*So do you,* thought Sarah, thinking of the flowered boots by the back door and the hat still hanging in the pantry.

"It's the TV," said Jep. "But if he doesn't have it, he gets restless. And there's nowhere he can go."

"What are you going to *do?*" asked Sarah, with her hand on the door handle.

He stood on the sidewalk, not moving. Then he made the barest shrug. "Keep feeding him," he said, and turned away.

She drove around the block and then she parked the truck and bent over the steering wheel and sobbed.

She cried for horror and for her poor dead carvings and for an old man who had lost everything and then had lost his wife too, who was left caring for a monster. She cried until her eyes were dry and burning and her nose ached and her forearms hurt where the steering wheel cut into them, and the world was still terrible.

Then, because she'd left the cash box there, and because some habits die hard, she went back to the flea market.

"You okay?" asked Rauf. "You don't look so good. What did he want, anyway?"

Sarah exhaled. Her throat was raw. "He showed me his workshop," she croaked "He doesn't carve since his wife died."

Rauf nodded.

"If my wife died," he said slowly, "I wouldn't do anything again. I'd just close up the shop and sit down and wait to see her again."

Sarah had met Rauf's wife two or three times, a small, round, dark-skinned woman with a smile that could light up a continent. She wondered if it was her smile that could make her husband want to do nothing but sit down and die if he lost her.

She wondered what Jep's wife's smile had been like.

"Hey, it's okay," said Rauf, seeing her face. "She'll outlive me. She'll do better without me than I would without her."

Sarah laughed dutifully and went into her stall. She threw her tools into her bag—all of them, and the paints too, which took three trips out to the truck—and dropped the half-finished ruddy on the passenger seat.

She went home to get the rest of her gear, and then through a drive-thru because she couldn't live on Rauf's popcorn all day.

And then she drove back to the little house with the painfully tidy yard and knocked on the door with her hands full of chisels and a bag of burgers.

Jep opened the door and blinked at her.

"Come on," she said. "I've brought my tools. Let's finish your horse."

Sarah thought, at some point in that mad night, that she had learned more about carving in the last five hours than she had learned in the fifteen years leading up to it. Her hands were nicked and bloody and her arms ached from holding the heavy wood at the proper angle. She did not have a vise remotely large enough, so they had to improvise with the table and the walls.

The years did not fall away from Jep's face, but his hands were younger than they had ever been. He stroked the tools over the surface of the horse and under the blades, the muscles came to shining life.

She knew that her tools were cheap, amateurish things compared to the woodshop he must have had, but he held them as if they belonged to a master.

When he passed her the knife and gestured to the horse's tail, she stared at him.

"Are you sure?" she said. "My ducks aren't that good..."

He stared down at the horse.

"The greatest thing I ever made came alive," he said finally. "Because I wanted to make my wife happy. And now she's gone and it sits there and I feed it and sometimes I dream about setting us both on fire."

Sarah's hand closed convulsively on the carving knife. She swallowed.

"You're a good girl," said Jep. He sounded tired. She knew that it must be very late. "I don't know if this will work. But I want you to know I'm grateful. And I'm sorry about all your decoys."

"It's all right," said Sarah, even though it wasn't.

She steeled herself, and began to carve the tail.

It was closer to morning than midnight when Jep cut the last hair on the back hoof. Sarah had been sanding the flanks until they gleamed under the shop lights.

He stepped back and looked at the horse.

"Yes," he said finally. "Yes, that's not bad."

There was a noise at the door.

They both looked up, and Sarah took a step back.

The marionette stood in the entryway.

*It's between us and the outside, what do I do, can we distract it...*

She moved so the horse was between her and the creature. If it came at them, it would have to move out of the doorway, and she could make a break for it.

*And what about Jep? He can't move that fast.*

"I locked the door," said Jep. "I always lock it."

The marionette rolled its carved eyes. "I've been able to open that lock for the last ten years."

Jep rested both hands on the horse's back. "I see," he said.

The wooden lips twisted up. "Are you surprised, old man? That I could open it, or that I didn't strangle you in your sleep some night?"

Jep shrugged.

The marionette looked down at the horse.

Its face changed. Sarah couldn't explain it. A light came behind its eyes that had been missing before.

It said, very quietly, "Oh."

It took a step forward and Sarah knew that she should be ready to run, but instead she burst out "Don't you dare try to eat this horse!"

The marionette laughed, but it wasn't the horrible clacking laughter that she had heard earlier. It was softer and more rueful, the most human sound that she had yet heard it make.

"I won't," it said. "I understand why you'd think that, but I wouldn't."

It took two more steps forward. Sarah backed up. Jep didn't.

It stroked one long, articulated hand over the horse's neck.

She could see the exact moment when the horse woke. She saw the flanks heave as it inhaled, and saw the marionette's ball-joint fingers tighten in the suddenly liquid mane.

"We did badly by each other, old man," said the marionette distantly.

"We did," said Jep quietly. "She'd have been disappointed in us."

It shook its head. "She'd have understood."

The horse lifted its head. Its carved nostrils flared open and it turned and nuzzled the marionette's arm.

"I'm going now," said the carved boy. "Finally. Now that I have my horse."

"All right," said Jep.

It—he—swung up on the horse's back. They were perfectly sized for one another. He had to lean far forward to go through the doorway, but then he was through.

As one, Sarah and Jep followed.

The moon was the eye of an ink-dark whale overhead, barnacled with stars. They walked through the shadows of the sideyard. The pale wood-grain color of the horse was bleached to blue-white bone.

Moonlight surrounded the boy and the horse as they walked into the street. The click of wooden hooves on asphalt became a clatter as the horse broke into a trot, and then into a run, and then the moonlight was a blue ribbon before them and they were running up it and there was no sound at all.

And they were gone.

Sarah had to put Jep to bed. He was heavy, for all his frailness, and she was practically carrying him as they reached the bedroom.

She tried to set him down on the near side of the bed and he struggled until she helped him around to the far side, where the blankets were pushed back. "My side," he said, by way of explanation. She looked at the other side, at the neatly tucked pillow and the faint depression in the mattress, and she would have cried again if there were any tears left in her.

She got his shoes off and left it at that. His frayed suit wouldn't get any more frayed for being slept in.

She picked up her tools. When she had duplicates, she left him one, and when she didn't she left him one anyway. Her credit card could strain to another few knives if they had to.

She let herself out of the shed and drove back to the flea market in the moonlight. She kept expecting to see a horse and a rider, but she didn't and she thought probably no one else ever would either.

She was exhausted, but there was no chance of sleeping. She didn't feel like going home.

Instead, she keyed in the security code and let herself into the empty building. Her stall was dark, but she turned on one light, and saw the reflections winking in Rauf's popcorn maker across the way.

She had the right tools to finish the ruddy, so she did.

There was light coming in through the skylights when she put the last line on the feathers.

She sat back. Her neck ached and her eyes were gritty. It was the best thing she had ever carved, even better than the horse's tail.

She didn't know what she was waiting for.

She set down the sandpaper and sighed.

"Maybe I'm being stupid," she said. Her voice sounded thin and lost in the vast echoing spaces of the market.

The duck carving flexed its wings. Its unpainted bill opened, just a fraction, and then it shook itself and settled back down. Its tail flicked, and then it was a wooden carving again, with no more life than any piece of art has on its own.

A single wooden feather slipped free of the wings and landed on the table.

She picked it up. It was unpainted, and more perfectly carved than anything that she had ever done.

But not, perhaps, more perfect than anything she *could* do.

She stroked her hands over the wood, then got up and turned out the light and went home.

# EDITING

I must remind myself—

they can't tell that I didn't write this bit immediately after that one

the six months where I ignored the manuscript are not visible to the naked eye

the bit where I put my head in my hands and muttered "I have no idea what I'm doing" takes place in the single space between the period and the next capital letter.

As soon as I shove that character in, she has always been there

and someone will probably say that she's the emotional center

and the book couldn't have been written without her

and nobody will know that I thought of her three thousand words from the end and scrolled up and shoehorned in a couple of paragraphs near the beginning because, for whatever reason, the story needed an elderly nun

she was almost the cook

and for about ten minutes she was the earnest young village priest

and now she has been there since you started reading.

I am sanding down the places where my editor found splinters

kicking up a fine dust of adjectives and dropped phrases

(Wear a breath mask. Work in a well-ventilated area. Have you seen what excess commas can do to your lungs?)

and eventually it will all be polished to a high shine

and hopefully when someone looks into it
they'll see their own face reflected back
instead of mine.

# BIRD BONES

The gardeners didn't notice it first, but they were the first ones that anybody took seriously.

The birdwatchers had been saying that birds were acting weird for months, but nobody listened, or if they listened, they assumed that the birds were acting weird because something was wrong with them, the way the crows had batted themselves against walls and windows when R-strain West Nile virus had come through and infected half the flocks in North America.

The Cornell Ornithology Lab put out a statement saying that peculiar flocking behavior was being observed in a number of backyard birds, causes unknown, but they didn't dare say what the behavior looked like, for fear of losing their funding. Some tree-huggers made hysterical claims about urban development driving birds insane, but people paid even less attention to them than the birdwatchers.

A number of homeless people in urban centers could have told Cornell some really astonishing things about the behavior of pigeons in recent months, but the homeless were considered only marginally more credible than the birdwatchers.

So it wasn't until the gardeners, who kept their birdfeeders stocked with bulk black oil sunflower and millet, had noticed it and started calling their local radio stations and TV stations and writing long letters to the editor that the rest of the world—slowly, grudgingly, and with a great many jokes—started to pay attention.

Louise sat on her back deck and watched the birds drill in formation over her garden.

She didn't know what else to call it. The sergeant, a hefty Carolina wren with a jaunty tail, sat on a fence post and shrilled orders, while flights of chickadees and titmice flew overhead in perfect wedges and chevrons. A red-bellied woodpecker clung to the bark of the big pin oak just over the back fence and drummed a measured march on the trunk.

Louise considered the possibility that she might be insane. It was possible, she supposed. She'd had to go on some pretty serious medications for her heart, and the list of side effects was a mile long and included things like "bladder rupture" and "sudden death." Hallucinations about military birds might have been on there, too. She'd stopped reading after the bit about sudden death.

The wren chirped a long liquid sequence, and three cardinals swept across the yard, surrounded by swirling clouds of chickadees.

Louise swatted at a mosquito. She'd forgotten to wear bug spray, as usual. A few years back, that would have been very dangerous—R-strain was no kinder to humans than to crows—but the sprays had been very effective. R-strain was wiped out in a single season. The usual sorts of people had complained about scientists playing god and there were still people claiming that little Timmy had become autistic after being bitten by a treated mosquito, but Louise was pretty sure they were full of crap. Some people would scream about anything with the word "vaccine" in it. Generally the same people who would buy anything with the word "organic" in it.

Another chirp, and the cardinals reversed direction, stacking themselves into a tight wedge. The chickadees broke formation and landed in a swarm in the holly bushes. A thin shriek of feathers announced the arrival of the mourning dove squadron.

There was a thud against the sliding glass door behind her. Pibb the cat had apparently noticed the avian display. Louise glanced back at him, and saw him scrabbling his paws against the glass, eyes huge.

"Leave it, Pibb," muttered Louise. "You're not getting out." The wren glanced at her briefly, then went back to calling orders.

The doves weren't very good. They kept falling out of time with the woodpecker, and they couldn't keep formation half as well as the cardinals. Louise could have sworn she heard the Carolina wren sigh, and as she watched, it lifted a foot and rubbed it across its forehead, as if it had a headache.

Two mourning doves collided. The *chik-a-dee-dee-dee*'s that came from the holly bushes sounded like sniggering.

Louise picked up her teacup. She was pleased to see that her hands weren't shaking at all. Apparently insanity was agreeing with her.

The wren gave up and uttered a flat, nasal chirp. The woodpecker stopped. The birds disposed themselves about the trees and bushes. A few landed on the birdfeeder and began squabbling over who got the best bit of seed.

She counted species—blue jay, dove, titmouse, chickadee, woodpecker, wren. There were goldfinches on the thistle feeder, although they hadn't taken part in the maneuvers, and a white-breasted nuthatch picking its way down a nearby pine tree. No grackles or robins, no house sparrows or house finches.

No crows. That was to be expected. She hardly ever saw crows any more. They had been hit terribly hard by the R-strain. She'd come out one morning and found that a flock had been in the trees over her property, and there were twenty-seven dead crows littering her deck and backyard.

She sighed into her tea. It had been terribly sad. Scary too, of course, but mostly just sad. Louise had put on rubber gloves and gathered them all up into a plastic garbage bag, crying the whole time. She'd barely pulled herself together long enough to call the county to come out and get the bodies. They'd been so limp, their glossy heads dangling when she picked them up, their eyes like bits of broken glass. Their beaks had punched holes in the plastic bag and she'd had to double and triple-bag them. It had been an awful morning's work.

She looked out at her backyard full of birds, who were indisputably alive. They didn't appear to be doing anything strange. Perhaps the hallucination had passed.

If it had been a hallucination, why had Pibb reacted? He'd seen *something* outside. He was still sitting at the glass, chattering his jaws the way cats did when they saw prey.

"Birds," muttered Louise to herself. "He saw birds, is all."

The Carolina wren hopped up to one of the uprights on the deck and sang *teakettle-teakettle-teakettle* at top volume, the way wrens always did. He probably weighed less than an ounce. Pibb was an indoor cat and weighed an insolent nineteen pounds, and no mouse set whisker inside the house without suffering immediate and violent death.

Louise would have put all her money on the wren.

Her tea had gotten cold. Louise went inside.

She noticed the next thing three days later. Normally she wouldn't have seen it at all—she usually went out to the Presbyterian church on Thursday afternoons, where they had a little bit of potluck and some singing. The singing was pretty bad, but the potluck was pretty good, so Louise figured it evened out.

This particular Thursday, however, she'd had a flat tire and had to get the car towed and by the time she paid the bill and got home—*eighty-nine* dollars! For a *tire!*—she was so cross and out-of-sorts that the thought of listening to thirty well-meaning people butcher "A Mighty Fortress Is Our God" was just too exhausting to contemplate.

She made a grilled cheese sandwich, looked at the liquor cabinet, looked away guiltily, grabbed a dill pickle spear, looked at the liquor cabinet again, then thought *Eighty-nine dollars!* and poured herself a rum-and-coke.

Balancing sandwich, pickle, and rum-and-coke, Louise shoved the sliding glass door open with her elbow, blocked Pibb's bolt for freedom with her foot, and slid out onto the back deck.

A shriek of rage and terror rang out behind her. She jumped, felt the sandwich plate slide, started to grab for it, felt her grip on her drink slip, and made an almost instantaneous cost-benefit analysis. Pickle and sandwich hit the ground. Louise looked down at the wreckage of her dinner, kicked pickle brine off her foot, and took a slug of rum-and-coke.

Then she turned around.

As she'd expected, it was Tilly.

Tilly was the neighbor's cat and Louise didn't much like him.

For one thing, Tilly had a habit of sitting just on the other side of the glass and taunting Pibb, who would work himself into a howling frenzy and run through the house, knocking breakable objects off end-tables and nightstands. This would have been reason enough to dislike Tilly, even leaving aside that he smelled bad and usually had fleas, because his owner, Mrs. Gothaway, was an irresponsible twit.

Worse, however, was the fact that bird-hunting was Tilly's religion. Louise had cleared all the cover around her birdbath and feeder, elevated the feeder five feet off the ground, and still he would kill them. Bluebirds, sparrows, fledglings in the nest—he'd bring home two or three a day sometimes, Mrs. Gothaway reported. She was proud of this fact, and there was no point suggesting a belled collar or trying to tell her about national declines in songbird populations. Mrs. Gothaway distrusted anything that resembled science or education and was proud of the fact that she had never voted in her life.

Louise, unfortunately, possessed a B.A. in mathematics, and somehow Mrs. Gothaway had learned this fact, with the result that she distrusted Louise as well, as if a seventy-three-year-old woman was going to descend on her in the night, tie her to a chair, and carve the quadratic equation into her back with a butcher knife.

Tilly shrieked again. He was not hunting birds. In fact, it looked like birds were hunting *him*.

Louise took another drink.

Three mockingbirds, in tight formation, were dive-bombing him when he tried to break for the woods. That wasn't particularly unusual—mockingbirds mobbed cats all the time, and hawks and crows and anything else they disapproved of.

What *was* unusual were the birds in the trees. They appeared to be using slingshots.

Louise set down her drink, slid the glass door open and fumbled for her binoculars, which she usually left on the end table by the door. She wasn't an avid birdwatcher—she didn't keep a list, and she wouldn't fly to some foreign country with bad plumbing just to see a strange bird—but she liked to know what she was looking at, and that meant keeping binoculars and a bird book within easy reach.

She found the binoculars, blocked another attempt by Pibb to visit the Great Outdoors, and focused in on one of the attackers.

It was a tufted titmouse, a little grey-and-white bird with a pointy crest and big dark eyes. It was standing on one leg and holding a very small slingshot with the other, pulling the strap—was that a rubber band? Looked like it—and a very small stone back with its beak. Then it opened its beak and left fly. Tilly yowled.

The titmouse fluttered down to the ground, picked up another tiny stone, then returned to its perch and took aim again.

Louise swept her binoculars through the trees. There were over a dozen birds visible, and probably more hidden in the leaves. They reloaded slowly, and their aim seemed to be erratic, but there were a great many of them, and the mockingbirds were keeping Tilly out in the open. Even if they didn't have enough force to cause real damage, the rocks had to sting. Tilly was spinning and yowling at every blow.

With her binoculars held firmly in place with one hand, Louise groped around for her rum-and-coke, found it, and drained it to the bottom.

She lowered her binoculars, wondering if it was worth it to try and find her camera, and Tilly caught sight of her and apparently thought that any human equaled salvation. He broke away from the mockingbirds, sprinted up the deck steps, and dove under a deck chair.

The mockingbirds looked at him, and then at Louise.

Louise gulped.

They flew towards her in tight formation, and landed one-two-three on the railing. They were less than four feet away. She could have taken a step forward and touched one.

They had hard bright eyes and their beaks looked suddenly menacing. Louise took a step back.

*This is ridiculous. A human afraid of a couple of mockingbirds!* It was like something out of that ridiculous Alfred Hitchcock movie. Louise had always thought the movie was stupid, since if the birds were going to run mad and kill you, sparrows and starlings were the least of your worries. A couple of angry swans could have taken out Tippi Hedren and crew in ten minutes, and spared everyone a lot of overacting.

Tilly hissed under the deck chair.

One of the mockingbirds let out a brisk *squark!* noise, and as one, the birds extended their left wings, dipped their heads, and *bowed* to Louise, as precisely as a team of Lipizzaners.

"Oh," said Louise out loud. "Oh. Goodness."

She tried to drink the rest of her rum-and-coke, discovered that she had already drunk it, thought vaguely that drinks just did not last as long as they had in her youth, and then, for lack of anything better to do, she bowed back.

"Always be polite. Bein' polite costs nothing," her grandmother had always said. Grandma had probably not been thinking of eerily intelligent mockingbirds, but it was good advice nonetheless.

She straightened up again. She wondered if they had really bowed—a primate gesture, a monkey gesture, wasn't it?—and whether returning it would make any sense to their tiny avian minds, or if they would construe it as a mortal insult and order the artillery flock to attack.

*And that I am even wondering this probably means that I have finally gone crazy. Completely around the bend. Oh dear.*

The mockingbirds took off again with a flip of their long tails and vanished into the trees.

She wondered if they knew the militant Carolina wren.

"I should tell someone," she said out loud. "I should…no, I can't, can I?"

If she were ten years younger, she would have called someone. The police, or the newspapers, or maybe her nephew. But she wasn't ten years younger, and people no longer spoke to her without the shadow of senility in their eyes.

"They'd put me in a home," she said glumly. "It'd be the Good Shepherd for sure." Where there were no birds—with slingshots or otherwise—but also no rum-and-coke, and the gardens were sad, stunted things with a lot of clipped boxwoods and no proper flowers.

"Waaaaoaargh," said Tilly.

"Uh-huh," said Louise. She inspected the mysteriously empty rum-and-coke. She should probably be a little drunk, but she felt deathly sober. She reached under the chair and hauled Tilly out by his scruff. "Let's get you home."

Tilly gave her a half-hearted scratch, but he was clearly a beaten cat. He hung limply the entire walk up Mrs. Gothaway's driveway.

The porch was covered in spiderwebs and broken yard equipment. Through the screen door, Louise could hear the sounds of a TV preacher promising hellfire upon the queers, the fornicators, and for some reason, the Amish.

She knocked on the frame of the screen door two or three times before she heard someone heaving themselves up from the chair inside.

"I'm comin'…"

Mrs. Gothaway appeared. She was skinny and bright-eyed, with knuckles like walnuts and nicotine stained fingers.

"I have your cat, Mrs. Gothaway," said Louise.

"I see that. Somethin' been after him?" She narrowed her eyes. "Dog? Coon?"

"Birds," said Louise, without thinking how that would sound.

*"Birds?"* Mrs. Gothaway stared at her as if she were crazy. "After *my* Tilly?"

"Um," said Louise hastily. "No, it was—ah—a big bird. Some kind of bird of prey, I think."

Mrs. Gothaway looked suitably horrified. "Well, I'll be. I'll tell Sonny to get his gun out. No bird's gonna mess with my Tilly!"

"No!" said Louise, horrified. Sonny Gothman was stupid, cruel, and perpetually unemployed. "Mean as a snake," Louise's grandma would have said. He was bad enough when he was out shooting mailboxes and drinking up his mother's welfare money—the notion of him shooting at living creatures, particularly the disturbingly intelligent, if undeniably courteous mockingbirds, gave Louise the creeping horrors.

The heavy lines around Mrs. Gothaway's mouth got heavier as she frowned. "You sayin' Sonny can't shoot a bird on his own land?"

"No," said Louise, thinking fast, "but if it was a bird of prey, it's illegal to shoot 'em. Sonny could get in trouble with the government."

This was the right thing to say. Mrs. Gothaway hated "the guv'mint" more than she hated just about anything, except maybe queers, fornicators and the Amish. Louise bore out the resulting five minute tirade, handed Tilly over, and beat a hasty retreat.

Louise seethed as she walked home. Couldn't be bothered to put a flea collar on the beast, couldn't be bothered to get him his shots, let him run around without getting fixed, siring half the unwanted kittens in the neighborhood, but let the cat get into a scrape that could be solved with firearms, and suddenly he was "my Tilly" and a valued member of the family.

"Ignorant old biddy," muttered Louise. "And I'm twice as bad, for thinking it would turn out any other way." *Why* had she said it was birds?

There was a story on the news that night, in the lighthearted "human interest" section that they aired after all the wars and stock-market crashes. A man who fed the ducks every day was attacked in the park by a feral dog. The ducks had turned on the dog and driven it away, saving the man from severe injury. In the interview, the man looked grateful but puzzled, and there was a hesitation to his answers that made Louise think that he might have found his ducks doing military drills across the pond recently.

"But of course you can't tell anybody," she said out loud to Pibb. "Because they'll think you're crazy. And since half the gardeners and birdwatchers out there are old people, we don't dare tell anybody, for fear they'll come and stick us in the home."

She wondered if anybody had said anything at the Garden Club meetings. She'd stopped going years ago, when the competition over bringing a perfect rosebud to the flower show had gotten so cutthroat that a ninety-two-year-old woman had been caught slashing her rival's tires with garden shears. Some of them wouldn't notice a herd of water buffalo in the garden, unless they suspected it of having designs on their dahlias.

Pibb rubbed against her shins. Louise sighed and went to bed.

She was up early the next morning, picking Japanese beetles off the roses. She only had two rosebushes these days. Cantankerous plants, roses, always getting weird little diseases and pests and scales, as if the world was never entirely to their liking. The hypochondriacs of the plant kingdom. They smelled beautiful when they bloomed, but they never bloomed long enough, and then, of course, you get beetles.

Japanese beetles are fat, copper-colored, and voracious. All you had to do was grab them, yank them off the leaf, and dump them in a bucket of soapy water. They're slow, lumbering beetles, so it's easy to do...unless, of course, you're seventy-three years old and not nearly as quick as you used to be.

She was having a bad day of it. The gloves made her clumsy, but she couldn't stand the way they squirmed against bare skin. She'd grab a joined pair of beetles—they were screwing all over the roses, disgusting things—and drop it in the bucket, but that would startle the others, and a dozen would take off from the bush, and she'd try to grab one out of the air and miss every time. Sometimes she even missed the stationary ones, and there was nothing to bring you down like being outwitted by a beetle.

She missed another one and said a word that would have shocked most of the members of the Garden Club. She managed to snag the next one, but she took a rose leaf with it and grumbled.

Something landed on her shoulder.

She turned her head, reaching a hand up automatically to brush away whatever it was, and froze. A bright black eye peered back at her, as the wren shifted its weight. She could see the fine scaly flesh around its eye, and the dusty feathers at the edges of the beak. There was something very reptilian about birds up close like that.

"Um," said Louise. "I'm....killing beetles. Um. Hello?"

The bird cocked its head and said "chuuurk!"

*Did I expect it to speak English?* For lack of any other ideas, Louise held up the Japanese beetle for the bird's inspection. It was a Carolina wren—the drill sergeant? Or another one? How could you tell?

It hopped down onto her upper arm and examined the beetle carefully. Most birds didn't eat Japanese beetles, that was part of the problem. Louise dropped it into the soapy water.

The wren hopped to the bucket, peered down into it, and then flew away. Louise exhaled.

*Well, what did you think would happen?*

She straightened up and set the bucket down. Her back twinged, and her left knee, which probably meant that the late spring weather was about to change.

The wren reappeared. It was carrying a kicking copper beetle in its beak. It landed on the edge of the bucket, dropped the beetle in, and looked up at her with bright eyes.

"Errr," said Louise. "Yes. Yes!" She nodded, and then thought *Nodding is stupid, it's a bird, it won't know what you mean.* Oh god, how did you communicate with a bird? All the primate gestures were useless. Heck, all the *mammal* gestures were useless. All those scientists worried about how you would communicate with space aliens, and the real question turned out to be how you communicated with a bird the size of an old woman's hand.

She reached out and grabbed another beetle and dropped it in the bucket.

The wren cocked its head again, and its throat vibrated briefly, and then it flew away again. She could hear it calling loudly in the shrubs.

A few minutes later, a female cardinal, clad in brown and orange, landed on the edge of the bucket and dropped a Japanese beetle into the water. The cardinal was followed by a pair of titmice, which were followed by a scruffy looking robin.

Louise sighed. It was going to be the Good Shepherd home for sure—but in the meantime, the roses were being spared. She went back to work, with the birds fluttering around her. She felt like a geriatric Snow White.

The bucket filled up with beetles.

After about twenty minutes, Louise straightened up, said "Excuse me," to the birds, and went inside. She got a drink of water, then opened her pantry and stood staring into it.

There was plenty of birdseed. But the birds had helped her—were helping her—and she felt like they deserved a treat. It's not like they could eat the beetles.

She found a half-full jar of peanut butter leftover from her turn bringing cookies to the pot-luck, and dug most of it out with a spoon, then dumped in some corn starch and some lard for good measure. Louise felt that it had been a sad day for the country when lard had been replaced by margarine, and anyway, birds didn't need to watch their weight.

She took the bowl of nutty goop outside and spooned most of it into the tray on the birdfeeder. The birds—who had still been cheerfully picking beetles off the roses—descended on the feeder with shrill chirps of delight.

"If you can take care of the roses, I'll bring you all the peanut butter you want," said Louise, thinking *No, doctor, of course I don't talk to birds, that would be crazy, why do you ask?*

"Chirrr!"

"Achicka-dee-dee-dee!"

"Teakettle-teakettle-teakettle!"

"Chee-ark! Chee-ark!"

On the news that night, the lighthearted story was about a jogger being trapped by a flock of feral parrots in Dallas. They'd kept him pinned down in an alley for six hours, until somebody brought in a pick-up truck load of fruit and seeds.

They interviewed a Cornell scientist, who explained about mobbing behavior in birds. "They were probably viewing him as a threat," said the ornithologist. "Fortunately, they were able to distract the birds with food, allowing the man to escape."

"Bleep!" said the jogger, interviewed directly afterwards. "Mobbing behavior my bleep! That was a hostage situation! Those birds weren't letting me go until they got their bleeping ransom payment!"

They cut back to the anchors, who joked about bird brains. Louise turned the TV off. Parrots holding joggers hostage was a far cry from her polite beetle-killers. "Well," she said to Pibb, "it's *Texas.* I suppose their birds are crazy too."

The gunshot rang out when Louise was taking a nap, which is why she ran outside in her bathrobe, white hair flying, one foot in a bedroom slipper and one, which had missed the slipper, completely bare.

At that moment, though she was less concerned about her appearance than the pathetic scatter of feathers under her birdfeeder.

"What are you *doing?*" she shouted.

Sonny Gothaway lowered his gun. He was leaning against the fence, and he had that "aw, shucks" look that dangerously stupid people sometimes get when they are trying to appear harmless. "Huntin' birds, Missus C. Mom says they went after Tilly."

"Not these birds!" Louise advanced on him. "You don't shoot *these* birds, you idiot!" Oh, *why* had she said it was birds? She should have said a possum got Tilly. She didn't wish harm to possums, but nobody ever accused a possum of being frighteningly intelligent.

Sonny narrowed his eyes, but Louise was too furious to pay attention to the warning signs. She marched towards him, shaking her finger. "It was a big bird that went after Tilly. Do these look like big birds to you?"

"You wanna be careful, Missus C," drawled Sonny, looking less harmless and more belligerent.

Some distant part of her brain was fully aware of how ridiculous she must look, marching towards him with one slipper and one foot covered in grass stains, her hair standing out in all directions and her bathrobe flapping around her bony knees. She didn't much care. If she'd been able, Louise would cheerfully have strangled him. The bird lying under the feeder had undoubtedly been more intelligent than Sonny, and it couldn't possibly have done as much harm in its entire life as Sonny managed in a week.

"You've got no call to be shooting birds on my property!" snapped Louise. Maybe that'd get through to him. His mother was always talking about *her* land and *her* property and let the guv'mint just *try* to take it.

Sonny pointed the gun at her.

Louise stopped.

About half of her was terrified. It was a very large gun. Louise didn't know anything about guns, couldn't tell a BB gun from an assault rifle, but it seemed *extremely* large.

The other half of her, unfortunately, was still furious, and it seemed to be in charge of her mouth.

"Don't you point that thing at me, Sonny Gothaway," she snapped. "You shoot me and the sheriff'll be out here in no time, goin' all through the woods, and even if they don't catch you, they'll find whatever it is you're doing back there that you think is so all-fired secret."

Sonny flushed. Louise had no idea what he was doing back there—in her youth, it was still moonshinin', and sometimes growing marijuana. Lord knew what kids got up to these days—crack or meth labs or growing opium poppies. Well, probably not opium poppies. Louise could grow poppies in her yard, but the heat usually flattened 'em come June, and Sonny just didn't seem like the type to hand-water a poppy and make sure it got a nice drink of compost tea twice a month.

Whatever it was, apparently Sonny was real surprised that people paid attention to little things like trucks coming and going at all hours of the night. "You wanna be careful, Missus C," he said again, but he sounded much less certain this time. "You wanna keep your mouth shut."

"Then you want to put that gun away," said Louise, jamming her hands on her hips and glaring at him.

He kept it pointed at her a moment longer, then spat over the fence and turned away. Louise watched him walk away until he was lost in the screening trees.

"Well," she said, and her voice cracked, and *then* the adrenalin hit her and she had to sit right down in the grass where she was. Her heart thudded in her chest. Was she having a heart attack? That'd be ironic.

She put her forehead on her knees and tried to breathe.

Something landed on her shoulder. She didn't need to look up to know that it was the wren.

*"Teakettle-teakettle-teakettle!"*

The voice of a Carolina wren is near-deafening at close range, particularly coming from such a small throat. Louise pressed her hand to her chest and said "It's okay. I'm fine. I'm fine. It's nothing."

The bird eyed her skeptically.

"I'm fine." She sighed. "Let's see about your friend..."

Sonny's victim was a female cardinal. There wasn't much left of her. Louise wondered if it was one of the cardinals who had helped her catch beetles. She felt sick and sad and old.

The wren perched atop the feeder and looked down at her. Louise glanced around the yard and saw titmice and mockingbirds, all watching her silently.

"I'll get the shovel," she said.

The ground was soft. It didn't take long. It took longer to gather up the drab red-brown feathers littering the grass, but Louise didn't feel right leaving them scattered across the yard. She put the sad little handful in atop the body of the cardinal, then filled in the hole.

The birds watched her the entire time. She wondered if they had any idea of what she was doing. Birds didn't bury their dead, did they? Did they realize she was trying to do what was proper for the cardinal?

*They probably think I'm saving her to eat later,* thought Louise gloomily. *Maybe they're wondering if they should all attack now, or maybe they don't care about their dead and are just wondering what's wrong with me.*

They didn't attack. Louise said the Lord's Prayer over the grave, for lack of anything else to say, and placed a rock on it. It joined the small stone-marked graves of Pibb's two predecessors and a mole that Louise had hit with her car four years previous and hadn't felt right just throwing into the woods.

The birds watched the whole process in silence. When she had said the last "Amen," a silence fell. Then a mockingbird sang—something sweet and sad and not entirely ruined by the addition of a car alarm imitation at the end.

That night, the birds began building something far back in the trees.

When the police officer showed up at Louise's door, her first, ridiculous thought was that they were there about the murder of the cardinal.

This was followed by the thought that police never do anything nearly so useful—witness the fact that Sonny Gothaway was still a free man—and she opened the door. In recent years, Louise had stopped feeling the vague unease that even law-abiding citizens feel in the presence of uniformed police. They were all just so *young.* The one on her stoop barely looked old enough to shave. What was he going to do, run her into the station on the handlebars of his bicycle?

"Ma'am?" said the policeman. "I'm Officer Daltry. I'm afraid you've been the victim of a nasty prank."

Louise blinked at him, and took a few steps onto the porch, looking for the rotten eggs or the soaped windows—did kids still soap windows?—or the rolls of toilet paper hanging from the trees.

"The mailman called us," said Officer Daltry patiently.

Louise sighed. "Did someone hit the mailbox with a baseball bat? You'd think that living on a cul-de-sac, they wouldn't, but some of these kids—"

"No, ma'am," said Officer Daltry, flushing. Apparently his training hadn't covered this particular scenario. "I'm afraid something's been left in your mailbox."

Louise raised her eyebrows. "Rotten eggs?"

"It was a dead possum, ma'am," said Daltry hurriedly.

Louise put a hand to her mouth.

It was Sonny—of course it was Sonny—fool boy, he thought he was scaring her. Well, she *was* scared, right enough, but she'd been scared anyway, so he'd wasted his time and some poor beast's life for it.

"That poor possum," she said. "I mean, you see them on the roads all the time, but it's different—in the *mailbox,* you say?"

"We're taking care of it," Daltry assured her, as she looked past him, down the driveway to the road.

"Oh. I suppose it's evidence, or something?" Louise tried to imagine Daltry taking a dead possum down to the station. Perhaps they had a cooler?

"We took photos," he said. "We, uh, didn't think you should have to see it."

Well, that was one nice thing about getting old. Police didn't make you clean dead animals out of your own mailbox. *If I was forty, I suppose they would simply give me a plastic bag and some bleach…*

"Thank you," she said. "Oh dear. How awful!"

"If you wouldn't mind—I need to take a statement—" Daltry pulled a boxy plastic clipboard. "Did you hear anything, ma'am?"

"Oh no," said Louise. She waved a hand to the distant mailbox. "I wouldn't have, though."

Daltry nodded. "Can you think of anyone who might have done this?"

*Sonny Gothaway,* she thought, but didn't say it. She didn't have any proof. You couldn't get fingerprints off a dead possum, could you? And if it was her word against his, they'd probably believe her—respectable retired math teacher versus young ne'er-do-well—but when you were seventy-three, you weren't exactly a reliable witness. What if they decided that Sonny Gothaway was harmless, and she was just a senile old biddy?

It would stir up a lot of trouble, and Sonny would be twice as bad. He might take it into her head to shoot *all* her birds. Sergeant Wren and the foolish doves and the courteous mockingbirds that had bowed to her. And how did you request police protection for a bunch of birds?

"I'm afraid I can't think of anyone who would do such a thing," said Louise to the police officer.

She went out that afternoon for groceries, and stopped by the liquor store for more rum. A rum-and-coke in the garden, she decided, was the best possible way to end a day. The Garden Club would have been shocked.

"Really, though," she said to the wren, who was sitting on the deck railing, overseeing maneuvers, "at my time of life, what am I saving my liver for?"

*"Teakettle-teakettle!"* agreed the wren.

Louise slapped at a mosquito, took a sip of her rum-and-coke, slapped another mosquito, and itched at spot where one had bitten her without being noticed.

"I don't suppose you can do much about mosquitos?" she asked the wren. "Or is that a bat thing?"

She hadn't noticed any bats behaving in eerily intelligent fashion, but a human probably wouldn't, would they? They could be doing madrigals and operettas in sonar, and nobody would be the wiser until some researcher pointed a microphone at them at the exact right moment.

"And he'd probably know better than to tell anyone," she told the wren. "They'd send him off to the Good Shepherd Home For People Who Listen To Bats."

Two doves collided in mid-air again. The wren sighed. Louise went inside for a citronella candle and some matches.

The wren watched her strike the match with great interest. "Chirrr?" It hopped down from the deck railing onto the little patio table and eyed the candle-flame.

"Be careful," said Louise. "I'm pretty sure feathers burn." She wondered how to illustrate the point, found a pine needle on the deck, and held it to the flame. The wren watched the little red line of fire creep up the pine needle. "Chirrrrr."

The scent of citronella wafted through the air. Louise leaned back in her chair and took another sip of her rum-and-coke.

"You din't ought to have called the cops," said Sonny Gothaway over the fence.

Louisa whirled around, feeling scared and furious and outraged at the sheer stupidity of what she had to deal with. "I didn't call them, you stupid boy!" she yelled, stumping toward him in her slippers. "You stuck the damn possum in the mailbox, and what did you think the mailman would do when he saw it? Stick the junk mail in between its toes?"

Sonny took a step back, plainly startled. A long red flush started on his meaty neck and ran up towards his ears. He wasn't carrying a gun, but a beer, she noted with some relief.

"For god's sake!" Louise threw her hands in the air. "You can't leave roadkill in somebody's mailbox and expect the mailman not to notice! If you're going to threaten me, stupid boy, think it *through* first!"

Really, crime was wasted on criminals. She would have been so much better at it than Sonny. It was a pity that she had lived such a blameless life.

*Me and Miss Marple...*

And that poor possum! Possums were no real trouble to anyone, as long as you made sure the lids on your trashcans were down tight. They were slow waddling beasts. You wouldn't want one as a pet, but why kill one?

Sonny threw the beer bottle at the garden gate before she reached it. The smash of glass was enough to bring her up short. In the sudden silence, she could hear the tinkle of tiny shards falling.

"You just better watch yourself," said Sonny, still beet red. "You just better watch what you say."

*Then don't stick any more possums in my mailbox*, Louise thought, but the words stuck in her throat. She would never in her life have thrown a beer bottle at someone. It would never have occurred to her to do so. She'd heard of couples who had screaming fights where they threw toasters at each other, and it always seemed like a waste of a perfectly good toaster.

Sonny turned and stalked away. Louise waited until she heard the screen door slam next door before stumbling back to the deck.

The grass was slick underfoot. She almost fell. Her stomach lurched as she lost her balance, and even when she caught herself heavily on the railing, she felt queasy and lightheaded.

That was the problem with getting old. You learned to be afraid of falling. The bones of an old woman were as brittle as the bones of a bird, without being given the gift of flight in exchange.

The wren landed on the railpost and chirped at her worriedly.

"I'm fine," she muttered. "Old and stupid, but fine."

The wren waited until she was at the sliding glass door before spreading its wings and zipping into the trees. Louise saw that the other birds had already vanished.

*Smart birds,* she thought, *they've learned to be afraid of Sonny. Smarter than me.*

She blew out the candle and went inside. It wasn't until the next morning that she realized the book of matches had vanished.

When Louise went into the garden the next morning, she peered through a crack in the blinds first, to see if Sonny had done something horrible. Then she was angry at herself for being fearful, and slammed the screen door back on its rollers so that it jumped the track at the bottom, and it took her five minutes and a lot of swearing to get it back in place. The Garden Club hadn't heard such language since Mr. Coolidge saw what the neighbor's lawn service had done to his prize Damask roses.

She took two steps out on the porch, armed with her morning cup of coffee, and her first thought was that Sonny had come back and dumped trash bags all over her yard.

Then one of the trash bags lifted its head and she realized that there was a flock of Canada geese in her garden.

"Oh lord!" said Louise. She liked birds, but Canada geese didn't really fall into that category, did they? They were more like airborne sheep. She could already see messy green droppings in the flowerbeds, and one of them had quite crushed a clump of spiderwort.

"Oh, *must* you?" she asked, going down the steps. "Not the spiderwort, please! Shoo! Go on!"

The goose heaved itself to its feet, but far from shooing, it glared at her and took a step forward. Its beak opened in a hiss.

It occurred to Louise that there were seven—no, eight—geese in the yard, and while she probably weighed more than all of them put together, the geese were nothing but bad temper and muscle. She took a step back toward the deck.

Three geese advanced in a wedge. One dropped its head and stretched its neck out, still hissing.

"Shoo?" she said again, but without much conviction. "Oh please, shoo!"

*Hisssss....*

Louise was wondering if she should throw the coffee cup at the leader and make a run for it, when the wren landed in the grass in front of the lead goose.

"Teakettle-teakettle-teakettle!" it shrilled, and then proceeded to read the goose the riot act (or so Louise guessed from the sound.) It chirped, it squawked, it paced back and forth and hopped up and down in apparent fury.

The Canada goose, abashed, snapped its beak shut and made a weak honking sound.

The wren gave another gruff chirp, puffing out its breast feathers. The Canada goose dropped its head back to its chest feathers and waddled slowly toward Louise.

"Honk," it said.

"It's okay," said Louise. "I—err—you just startled me is all."

"Honk." It bobbed its head at her several times, then turned and lurched across the grass into the flowerbeds. Louise sighed.

"Friends of yours?" she asked the wren.

"Chirr."

"My garden really isn't cut out for geese, you know. I mean, I don't *mind,* I guess—although I do, sort of—but—I don't even have a pond. The birdbath will fall over if they try to—oh, it already has. I see."

The wren flipped its tail and began preening under one wing.

Louise went back into her house to add a shot of whiskey to her coffee. Perhaps if she simply bookended the day with drinks, it would all work out. She found the remains of a loaf of bread, which she had planned to make into croutons, but which would probably do okay for feeding geese. She brought it out, tearing it into small chunks.

The geese lined up politely, single file, and marched toward her. The first goose reached out and plucked the bread from her fingers with incredible delicacy, bobbed its head at her, then stepped aside and went to the back of the line. The next one stepped forward for its share.

Louise began, for the first time, to really feel as if she might have lost her mind. This was not goose behavior in any world that she understood.

Each goose got at least two pieces of bread. When she was done, there was a chorus of polite honks, and the geese dispersed back into the garden, settling themselves in brown and cream lumps. The spiderwort got trampled again. Louise didn't feel the need to comment on it.

Sonny Gothaway opened the gate to that interfering old cow's garden at about eleven that night. The moon was bright enough that he didn't need a flashlight, even though he'd brought one just in case. He wasn't real worried about the old lady being up to see him. She was—what, a hundred or so? She probably fell asleep right after Matlock.

He was pissed. The cops had been poking around for two days now, and Dan said that they'd driven right by the shed. They hadn't stopped, but they'd slowed down, like they were thinking about it. It was that stupid old lady's fault, calling them out just because of a possum in her mailbox, when she ought to have known it was there to keep her damn mouth shut.

Sonny was not by any measure intelligent. He got an idea in his head about how something would go, and if things did not proceed as he expected—due to unforeseen entities like mailmen or police—his tendency was to become enraged at the people who failed to behave in the way that that they were supposed to.

Since the mailman generally did his rounds before Sonny even got up in the morning, the other two principles in this drama were the police and the old lady. Sonny couldn't hate the police any more than he did, but since it was old Louise that brought the police down on him—well, he wouldn't be surprised if she'd told them all about his operation back in the woods. Nosy old bitch. It was pure spite, too—it wasn't like he was running a meth lab in *her* yard. Some people just couldn't let the small businessman well enough alone.

"Bad move, Missus C," he muttered under his breath. "Bad-fucking-move."

Well, he'd fix her up. She was like a million years old, and nobody'd be surprised when she turned up dead. They wouldn't even find the body for a week. Probably the cat would eat her.

This thought pleased him. Ordinarily he might have thrown her cat down the stairs just on principle, but if the cat ate the body, well, that was one more thing to keep the police from thinking it might be a murder. He'd planned to just put a pillow over her face and hold her down, but maybe he ought to cut her up a bit afterwards, just to get the cat interested. It'd probably make the news as one of those gruesome stories about why old people should be in homes, not dying and rotting in the house alone. Lord, Dan would laugh.

He climbed the back stairs to the deck—one creaked a bit, but who could tell, with the frogs and the crickets making so much racket?—and slipped a hand in the pocket of his jeans. Sliding glass doors were easy as hell to jimmy. You just needed a flat bit of metal, and of course the old lady hadn't put a dowel in the bottom to wedge it closed. Bending over like that probably hurt her hip.

Sonny had just gotten the glass door open when he heard something behind him, shockingly loud.

"*Teakettle-teakettle-teakettle!*"

He spun around, fist raised—and saw a bird.

"Oh, for fuck's sake..."

It wasn't even a big bird. It was a little scrawny thing with a sticky-up tail, standing on the post and yelling at him.

It cocked its head and let out that clattery yell again. Even a deaf old lady could probably hear that.

Sonny took a step towards it, waving his hand. "Get out of here!" he hissed. "Shut up, you little bastard!"

He swung at the bird. It leapt out of the way and landed farther down on the railing.

"Teakettle-teakettle-teakettle!"

"Stupid bird..." He took another step forward, coming out from under the overhang of the roof.

Hot pain scalded the back of his head, as sudden and shocking as a snakebite. Sonny let out a yelp and jerked back, actually hitting his head on the wall, which shocked him all over again.

He had to turn the flashlight on to be sure, but the darkness on his fingers was blood. Blood! Something had hit him and vanished again!

He looked around wildly—was it the old lady? Had she cracked him over the back of the head somehow? No, the glass door was only cracked open a half inch, and the house was dark and silent. What the *fuck...*?

Something honked at him from the garden.

He swept the flashlight over the ground and saw a goose.

Sonny Gothaway was neither intelligent nor a birdwatcher, and so did not stop to think that a goose was not nearly maneuverable enough to attack him from the air, and did not have much in the way of talons anyway. The goose was alive, it was there, and Sonny was mad and in pain.

He charged down the stairs and after the goose. It waddled away frantically, skidding through the garden gate barely ahead of him, and he lost sight of it for a moment. A honk from the gravel road alerted him, and he saw it, waddling foolishly down the drive, its tail waggling from side to side.

Louise and the glass door were briefly forgotten. At the moment, all Sonny Gothaway could think of was charging up behind the goose and drop-kicking it.

He took three long strides and was practically on top of the stupid bird when something went for his face again. Sonny staggered hard to one side—god, did it have *knives?* What the hell was going on?

He caught a glimpse of his attacker this time, winging away into the darkness. It wasn't a goose. It was one of those freaky owls with a face like a deformed monkey. His head was hot and sticky, and there was a big flap of skin waggling back and forth over his right ear.

The bastard had practically scalped him! What was wrong with it?

Honking caught his attention again, but he was no longer interested in the goose. He waved his flashlight through the trees, trying to catch a glimpse of the owl again. If it came for him again, he'd twist its freaky deformed *neck.*

"Teakettle-teakettle!" called the little brown bird, from somewhere in the trees.

He couldn't shake the feeling that the birds were working together. Were they some kind of pack, like dogs? Did birds even do that?

His shed was another few hundred yards down the road. Maybe he should go there. The birds sure couldn't get inside, and maybe a little meth would clear his head. Besides, if he came in covered in blood, his mom would freak the fuck out, start demanding he go to a hospital or some shit, and that never went well. Sonny didn't think there were any outstanding warrants for his arrest, but you never knew when the cops would pull something up out of spite.

He was partway down the road when the owl hit him again. This time he was ready. He swung the flashlight up toward the bird, and it veered off with a clawful of hair.

*Stupid bird, ought to know better than—*

The second owl got him in the side of the head, driving him off the road and taking most of his left ear with it.

Sonny Gothaway went to his knees, dropping the flashlight. He began to crawl away from the road. There was no thought in his head except to get away from those insane owls who'd lost their mind and had bird-rabies or some shit, and looked to kill him before he'd gotten back to the shed.

He'd made a couple of yards when he heard it again—"Teakettle-teakettle-teakettle!" and ran into something with his shoulder. It was twigs—branches—some kind of brush pile or something. Maybe he could put his back to it and keep those fucking owls from hitting him from behind.

A match struck, and he looked up.

The flame went out almost at once, but in that brief instant, he saw an outline over his head, a stylized shape with an enormous arching neck and a sharp beak.

A giant bird? What the *fuck...?*

A hot weight hit the back of his neck, and then two bands of shadow swept in on the sides of his peripheral vision, slamming into the sides of his head, and Sonny Gothaway lost consciousness immediately.

"Ma'am?" said Officer Daltry. "I'm sorry to bother you. I wanted to know if you'd seen any smoke in the last few days?"

"Smoke?" Louise leaned her cheek against the doorframe. "Smoke…sorry, young man, no. Somebody's always burning leaves or having a bonfire somewhere, so I wouldn't have noticed unless there was a lot of it. Why?"

If Officer Daltry objected to being called "young man," he didn't show it. "I'm sorry, ma'am, this may come as a bit of shock to you. We're investigating a murder."

"A murder," said Louise blankly.

"Have you seen a man named Sonny Gothaway recently?"

"Not for a few days," she said cautiously. "Did he murder somebody?" She grimaced. "He's always been a bad sort, I'm afraid, and I can't say it would surprise me—"

"No, ma'am," said Officer Daltry. "I'm afraid he's the one's been murdered." He rubbed his forehead and Louise felt suddenly sorry for him. He was so young.

"Would you like some coffee, officer? You look about done in."

He smiled faintly. "I'd be glad of it, ma'am. It's a nasty mess out there, and we're going to have people from the FBI all over the place, and probably reporters as well, so I have to come and tell everybody in the area what to expect."

"Of course you do," said Louise. She opened the door for him. "You come sit down a minute, and tell me whatever you can tell me. Although—" she added, over her shoulder, "I have to tell you that I never liked Sonny, and I can't say I'm sorry he's dead."

Daltry gave a short little laugh. "You're not the first person to say so, ma'am."

"Was it something with—whatever that business was that had people driving back there at all hours?" asked Louise, pouring them both a cup of coffee. "And do you take cream or sugar?"

"Black, ma'am, and thank you. We don't know, I'm afraid. He had a meth lab back there—I'm sorry, do you know meth labs? They're—"

"Young man," said Louise, with some asperity, "I may be old, but I still watch the news. I have heard of meth labs! Nasty things, aren't they? Don't they explode?"

"They can," Officer Daltry allowed.

"So that's what Sonny was doing. Well, I'm not surprised." She sat down. "No, that's not true. I'm surprised he was smart enough to do that. He never seemed bright enough to fool about with chemicals. So did his meth lab explode?"

"I'm afraid it was stranger than that," said Daltry. "Someone built a kind of structure—looks almost like wicker, or a bird's nest or something—in the shape of a bird, and stuffed him inside it, and then set fire to it. It didn't burn very well, but the coroner says he was unconscious and the smoke got him. We were hoping someone saw the smoke, but…well…"

Louise put a hand over her mouth. "How awful!"

Daltry took a slug of coffee. "We can't give out any details, of course, but it'll be all over the news in a few hours. The FBI will probably come by in a day or two to get a statement from you."

"Of course," said Louise. "The FBI—oh dear! How awful to have happen here!" She stared into her coffee. "Poor Mrs. Gothaway. She's not worth much, you know, but she did love him, I think."

Officer Daltry nodded.

"Did he—did he suffer much?"

"No, ma'am. Somebody hit him over the head first, and he probably never woke up at all."

"Oh," said Louise faintly. "That's good." She thought she should probably care more than she did, but all she could think of was the pitiful little body of the female cardinal.

Officer Daltry misread her concern. "Ma'am, I wouldn't worry too much. Most of the time with things like this, it was a bad drug deal, and the other guy tried to make the crime scene look like some kind of Satanist crap to throw us off the scent. They watch too much TV. We'll have a patrol car in the area, but we don't think anybody local is in danger."

"That's good to know," said Louise.

"Anyway, ma'am, I should be going. Are you going to be available for the FBI?"

"Oh, of course! I wasn't going anywhere." Louise paused, suddenly alarmed. "I'm not—oh dear, not a suspect, am I?"

Daltry laughed at that. "No, ma'am. Whoever hit him cracked him on both sides of the head, and gave him a one hell of a concuss—" He stopped and cleared his throat. "Well, anyway, ma'am, if you'll forgive me for saying so, we're looking for someone who could overpower Gothaway, and I don't think you're high on our list of suspects for that."

Louise smiled. "No offense taken, young man. Do you need a warm-up on your coffee? No? All right. Please come back any time—if you're tramping around in those nasty woods at all hours and getting chilled, I'll leave the pot on for you."

"Much obliged, ma'am."

Louise stood on the front porch and watched him walk down the driveway, headed to the next set of neighbors. No, she wasn't a suspect. Nobody in their right mind would think that an old woman could overpower Sonny Gothaway.

She went out on the back deck. The wren chirped at her cheerfully, and she lifted a hand in salute. Her roses, completely free of Japanese beetles, released an elegant perfume into the air.

There had been several enormous flight feathers on the deck three days ago, from the wings of a Canada goose. Louise had read that a swan could break a man's leg with its wing. She wondered what effect a goose's wing could have on a man's head. (The geese had, thankfully, flown away yesterday evening, leaving a great many green piles behind them. Her spiderwort would probably never be the same.)

It had rained heavily two nights before, which had nicely eliminated any tracks left in the yard. She'd had to use Clorox on the bloody smear that the back of Sonny's head had left on the wall. It wasn't likely that the FBI would be swabbing her vinyl siding, but you just never knew, did you?

She'd had a pretty good idea that something had happened when she'd found the sliding glass door ajar. Pibb had been absolutely frantic, but he couldn't get the door open the extra inch that would let him fit his fat belly through the gap.

That weird little bit of metal that she'd found on the deck had gone into a box which had gone into the very back part of the attic, under the tangled Christmas lights and an old box of National Geographics.

She wondered, idly, if the birds had done it purely in self-defense, or if they had been making some kind of offering to unknown avian gods. A giant wicker nest, set on fire…well, you had to wonder. The newspapers were full of speculation about the birds these days, ranging from a side-effect of the R-strain West Nile vaccine, to a judgment from God. Somebody on FOX News had said that the birds were possessed by demons and the end times were upon the earth, but then again, they said that whenever there was a hurricane or a Democrat in the White House.

For her part, she preferred to think that it was a kindness. A favor done in return for a great deal of birdseed and occasional bits of peanut butter.

"I suppose it's all for the best," said Louise. "They'll figure you out eventually. And you'll always be welcome in my garden—but you know that, don't you?"

"Chirr," said the wren agreeably.

# THAT TIME WITH BOB AND THE UNICORN

*I went to sushi with a friend of mine and tried to explain this idea to her—which mostly involved me saying "Bob, virginity is a cultur-al con-struct," in a bad Southern accent—and she told me that if I didn't write it and send it to her, she would hunt me down. I would rather like to know more about the good doctor, honestly, who seems like a good person to have around.*

So I was at the coffee shop the other day and I ran into Bob—not the Reverend, but Marlene's boy—and he was talking about unicorns.

I don't talk to Bob all that much, but being retired, I do spend a lot of time down at the coffee shop, partly so that I don't get weird from being home alone all the time and partly because my niece Donna got me a fancy coffee maker and I've read the manual twice and I still don't know how to use it. But she's my favorite niece so I keep it out on the counter for when she comes to visit and I get all my coffee down at the coffee shop.

Anyway, Bob was going on about unicorns and how he aimed to catch himself one, for reasons that I was none too clear on myself. And I could see two problems with that right off, so I said "Bob, aren't unicorns mythical?" and he said no, he was pretty sure they were just real sneaky, but he had a sure-fired method that was going to work, which was to get a virgin and sing a song he'd got from a book, and then he proceeded to sing a few bars and that was really all I needed to hear, though I assume the unicorns would have appreciated it.

So then I brought up the other problem, which was that Bob is definitely not a virgin, which I do not know from personal experience, you understand, but because everybody knows he pays child support to a woman over in Buncombe County, and we all know it because he talks about it on his Facebook page practically every day and posts a lot of tirades about how women are sucking the pioneering spirit out of men and the courts are all rigged against fathers and if women's lib was really a thing, how come we don't draft women?

I'd unfriended him quietly awhile back, and mostly relied on Marlene to tell me how he was doing. I respect everybody's right to post stupid-ass screeds on their Facebook, but I don't want to try and read it before breakfast. You start the day looking at that and you spend all day itching for a fight. I like to start with some pictures of tiny kittens who've made friends with big dogs and then maybe some science articles. It's amazing how much science I've been able to catch up with, being retired.

But anyway, Bob showed me a ring he was wearing and said that it was a symbol that he'd undergone a re-virgining ceremony where he dedicated his life to purity and now he was a virgin again, which I guess is a thing you can do these days.

"But Bob," I said, "virginity is a culturally constructed category," and then I explained to him about how being a virgin in different cultures meant that sometimes you were a virgin 'til you married or 'til you had kids and if you were an Ancient Egyptian, you didn't even have a concept of virginity at all. He was starting to get a little fidgety about that point, though, so I stopped with the Ancient Egyptians even though I think it's fascinating and I explained that he needed to make sure the unicorn had the same cultural concept of virginity as he had, and if that involved re-virgining then he was maybe gonna wind up with an evangelical unicorn, not that this was necessarily a problem if it was what he was going for, but you like to know what to expect.

But Bob was convinced he'd figured it all out and he finished his coffee and left off and I read an article about what that probe on Pluto found out and then another one about a momma pig that adopted a whole bunch of little baby ducks.

Anyway, I went out of town for a bit and what with one thing and another, I didn't see Bob for a couple of weeks, and when I got back into the coffee shop, there he was, hunched over a cup of coffee like a hawk with a hangover.

So I asked him about how his unicorn hunting went and he gave me a look and he said that I'd know if I bothered to follow him on Facebook.

"Bob," I said, "we have been over this ground before. There is an acceptable ratio of cat pictures to screeds about men's rights and you have reversed the numbers on that par*tic*ular ratio, and that is why I don't plan to friend you again. So what happened with the unicorn?"

He gave a hollow sort of laugh, like a mortician who's heard the same joke too many times before and he said he'd got himself a narwhal.

"A narwhal!" I say.

"A narwhal," he says. Apparently he'd been sitting in the pool singing the unicorn song with the re-virgining ring in the water and WHAM, there was a narwhal cuddling up next to him, as best one could given the size of the pool and the size of the narwhal and the size of Bob.

Well, that was not one of the ways I had pictured Bob's unicorn hunting going—my money'd been on him shooting himself in the foot, actually, like the time he took out after a snipe, except the other foot this time, for symmetry's sake. But when I stopped and thought about it, it did make a certain kind of sense, if you start off by thinking that maybe unicorns aren't a thing themselves, but a condition that happens to your hoofed mammals, like some of them being born white with blue eyes. And then you figure that you get unicorn horses and unicorn cows and some of those unicorn gazelles over in the desert where they got all the stories about evil antelope unicorns, and of course whales are all descended from hoofstock that went back into the ocean a shit-ton of time ago, pardon my language, but I don't think you can really express geologic time properly without profanity and you figure that maybe that *Ambulocetus* what they call the "walking whale" took the unicorn genes with him and if it happened a bunch and they all swam around together and kept marrying their cousins the way you're not supposed to do, you'd get your narwhals eventually.

I tried to explain this all to Bob, and even went so far as to draw out an *Ambulocetus* on a napkin, but I could tell he wasn't all that interested, even though it was a pretty good drawing, if I do say so myself.

"Bob," I say, "a man who is no longer interested in the genetics of inbred hillbilly water unicorns is a man who is no longer interested in *life.* I am afraid for your priorities, son."

"Fine," he says, "but that doesn't change the fact that I got a narwhal in my above-ground swimming pool, now does it?"

"Bob," I say, "that is *animal cruelty.* You cannot keep a narwhal in an above-ground swimming pool. They are cold-water animals and the chlorine can't be good for them."

"I've been feeding it frozen fish sticks," he said, and I vowed then and there to save that poor narwhal, which deserved a whole lot better than Bob.

So I finished my coffee and I went home and I called up Donna, my niece, who is still a virgin on account of her being one of those gold-star lesbians, which I know because she talked about it on her Facebook page and I was most of the way into the post before I realized what was going on. She posts a pretty good ratio of cat pictures to screeds so I hadn't been expecting it at the time. Donna answered the phone, and I explained about Bob and the narwhal first, so she wouldn't think I was asking for a weird reason, and then asked if she was still one of those gold-star lesbians, and she allowed how she was, but she didn't talk about it online any more in case it was insensitive to people who'd taken a bit of a different path to get where they were going.

"Right," I said, "I need your help because I think I need a virgin to soothe this narwhal who's been traumatized," and she asked how it had been traumatized and I reminded her about when she'd gone on a blind date with Bob back when she was in the closet and she slammed down the phone and was coming down the driveway before I'd finished talking. I barely had enough time to throw the coffee pot into the sink so it looked like I'd been using the coffee maker she got me.

(A couple months after all this went down, I learned that narwhals are like the Ancient Egyptians and don't have a cultural concept of virginity, which would have made things a whole lot easier, but none of us knew it at the time, and hindsight's a bear. But I still would have called Donna anyway, since she's my favorite niece.)

So I got out the Buffalo then, which is what I call the truck my mother left me, because of the time I went to Namibia and saw the African buffalo which are fearless and charge without warning and kill more people than any other animal on the continent and as it happens all those things also described my mother driving her truck, so the name stuck. The Buffalo's still in good shape for its age, and Donna followed me in her little Subaru and we went out to Bob's place and went around back and there was the poor narwhal stuffed in the aboveground pool like a dog in a toilet.

It was obviously in a pretty bad way, what with the heat, and I can't imagine the fresh water made it too happy—not that you could call it fresh when it was full of narwhal turds like it was—so I did not feel any qualms about relieving Bob of his ill-gotten narwhal while he was at work.

We backed up the Buffalo to the pool and getting the narwhal into the bed of the truck was a mess that I won't bore you with, even though I'd brought a tarp and a winch. It took a couple of hours, even though the narwhal figured out what we were doing and was eager to help. It was pretty easy to see that it'd gone off

Bob, which happens to nearly everybody eventually, although in retrospect I can't imagine the narwhal had Facebook.

So anyway, we finally got the narwhal into the pickup bed and Donna was real bitter because we'd torn her bumper off in the process, although I promised I'd replace it, and then we had to stash the Subaru down the road so that she could ride in the bed with the narwhal and keep hosing it down. I'd put a couple of coolers full of ice cubes in the bed of the Buffalo, and it was clear that the narwhal appreciated it, although the problem with beached whales as I understand it is that their internal organs get so heavy that they can't breathe all that well, and I couldn't do anything about that while it was in the pickup.

Donna banged on the window and asked where we were going and I said the aquarium up in Nag's Head, since the ASPCA didn't have much in the way of facilities for unwanted narwhals and she was skeptical that they'd just let us dump a narwhal at the aquarium, but I said it'd be fine. They know me up at the aquarium, and they've been real friendly ever since my mother died and we spent a lot of her money from the wrongful death settlement to build them one of those centers where little kids can come in and pet starfish in the big shallow tanks. She'd always loved that story about the little boy and all the beached starfish and he keeps throwing them back even though there so many of them, and the moral is that even if you can't save everybody, you can make a difference for individuals. Mom made a difference herself for a lot of individuals, many of whom would have maybe preferred to be left undifferentiated, so it seemed appropriate. It was called the Phyllis T. Williams Hands On Learning Center, hands-on learning being another one of those things that Mom practiced frequently and to the detriment of others.

"I don't think they're gonna let you dump a narwhal on them," she said.

"It'll be fine," I said. "I am a member of their Platinum Leadership Council," which is true because that's what they call you if you give them enough money, as opposed to their regular Leadership Council, which is if you only give them enough to hose the oil off a couple of unfortunate sea turtles.

So we rolled up to the aquarium and sure enough, the back door was open and the head director was out there and he was real nice and shook hands with everybody and called me "Doctor Williams," which hardly anybody does these days since I'm retired.

A little bit of the niceness sort of oozed off him when he looked in the back of the pickup and saw Donna icing down the narwhal, and he got a funny expression like a man who has just stepped in something and is afraid to look down and see what it might be, and then he wanted to know if it was a stolen narwhal and I am afraid I lied and said that narwhal had been a voluntary surrender and then I was a little bit nervous because I could feel it going bad so I spun him a story about a friend who hadn't gotten his narwhal spayed and now there was a litter but he'd found good homes except for this one and I don't think he believed me on account of that being a monumentally stupid story but he also didn't want to call one of the Platinum Leadership Council people a liar to their face, just in case I was looking to die myself and leave them money for a black-light jellyfish tank, which was what they were currently trying to fund according to the newsletters that they occasionally sent out to the house. (I don't know why the jellyfish needed a black-light, unless they were trying to appeal to the local stoner demographic and get kids in there watching jellyfish and listening to *Dark Side of the Moon*, which would admittedly be pretty cool, when you think about it.)

Anyway, the narwhal let out a groan then, like a cow giving birth to a cinder block, and the head director decided maybe stolen narwhals were bad but letting a narwhal die out back of the aquarium was going to look real bad in the papers, so they rolled the narwhal onto the gurney they use for their belugas and hustled it inside. Donna went along to keep the narwhal calm, but I stayed outside and talked about how I'd always been a big fan of both

Pink Floyd and jellyfish conservation, and eventually Donna came back and gave me the thumbs up.

So I wrote the man a check and that is why there is now the Doctor Williams Jellyfish Experience at the aquarium, to the left when you walk in.

They called me up a few months later to ask if I could get another narwhal, on account of them trying to breed the one we'd delivered, and I tried to volunteer Bob to magic up another one, but he wouldn't have any of it. Said he'd gone and re-de-virgined himself, and I'd have known that if I followed his Facebook page. I told him that if he was putting that sort of thing of Facebook, I was doubly glad not to be watching it. Marlene says he's interested in frogs now. I kind of feel sorry for the frogs, but I imagine they'll be a lot easier to transport if push comes to shove.

I wrote up my theory about unicornism as a magical genetic expression in ungulates and sent it off to a nature journal, and they say they're going to publish it, which is nice. I even made a little money of it, though not nearly enough to pay for the Doctor Williams Jellyfish Experience. But you know, I'm just glad I've had so much more time to do these sorts of things, now that I'm retired.

# RAZORBACK

*The story of Rawhead and Bloody Bones originated in Europe but migrated to the American South and underwent a local transformation. The definitive folklore version is likely S. E. Schlosser's and is very much worth reading on its own.*

There was a witch who lived up in the mountains, and I never heard but that she was a good one.

Some people will tell you she was old, but I don't think she was. She just had one of those faces full of lines. With a face like that, you look a lot older than everybody else, but as time goes on, they all look older and you don't, and you end up looking younger than everybody else by the time you die.

And you do learn early on not to get by on your looks, so there's that.

I never did learn who her people were or if she had any. A whole lot of people wound up in the mountains—Lumbee and Cherokee and escaped slaves and the grandkids of people who lit off into the hills for one thing or another. Little bitty scraps of this group and that, all of 'em living together and having kids. Leftover people.

She was one of those. Most of us were, one way or another.

The witch had a couple of names, depending who you ask, but everybody in town called her "Sal." She wasn't the only witch there, I'll tell you right now, but she was the best of the lot.

If you went south and east from town, you got into the sand-hills, where the rain runs down through the dirt without ever stopping, and there was a witch out there named Elizabeth Gray. Her heart was as dry as the sand and things ran through it without ever stopping. She couldn't be moved by pity or anger, and she only dealt in cash.

If you went north, you'd run into the river, and there was a shack down on the riverbank and an old woman lived in it who was madder than a shoe. She'd have had to come a long way to just be senile. She believed she was a witch and she'd cast a curse for a slug of whiskey and a couple of cigarettes, but whether the curses did anything much, I couldn't tell you.

(They do say that the sheriff riled her up and she cursed him and that's why he took a nail in the foot and got sepsis and his daughter ran off with a horse-thief. If you ask me, though, the nail was bad luck, and his daughter was fixing to run off with the first person who looked at her twice. But I don't know, maybe it was the woman from down on the mudflats.)

Sal, though … Sal was good. She never promised what she couldn't deliver, and she wouldn't ill-wish somebody just on a customer's say-so. She wouldn't brew up a love potion, but she'd cook up a charm to make a girl look a bit better or to give a bit of fire back to a man who was down to the last of the coals, if you understand what I'm saying.

And if somebody got a little too much fire in their belly, well, Sal knew how to make some unexpected surprises go away, too. That didn't put her in good order with the preacher, but preachers aren't traditionally fond of witches anyhow, so she didn't lose much by it. You didn't get so many girls in our town going to visit relatives for a year and turning back up with a baby and a tale of a dead husband, either.

Now, you'd think that somebody who provided this sort of community service would live in the middle of town in a house with glass windows, but you'd be wrong. Sal lived halfway up a mountain in a tumbledown house with a porch like a cow's hipbones. It was a long trek out to see her, and that was the way she liked it. She didn't have many friends to be inconvenienced by the walk. People want a witch when they need one, but they don't much like them. It was a little too easy, when you saw Sal go by, to remember what all she knew about you.

She didn't make it easy for anybody, either. She'd catch your eye and smile a little, and you'd remember that little matter she took care of for you and know that she was remembering it, too.

She was a good witch and a decent person, but decent people aren't always easy to live with.

So at the end of the day, Sal's best friend was a razorback hog.

He was a damn big animal, size of a pony. Some idiot over by Graham got the bright idea to bring in boars for rich people to hunt, thinking he'd keep them fenced up in a park, and of course there were boars on either side of the fence before you could say "Well, that's a stupid goddamn idea, isn't it?" So this razorback's granddaddy was a boar from the old country. Sal used to say he could see the fairies and liked to dig up their nests and gulp 'em down whole.

She called him "Rawhead." If you've ever seen the hogs down at the butcher shop, before they make headcheese, you know what she was talking about. They take the skin right off and what you've got left is a bloody skull with teeth like tent pegs.

Rawhead turned up one day in the garden and started rooting around in her compost heap. He had a taste for magic and there was plenty of it there, alongside the eggshells and the wishing melon rinds. (I never met a witch worth her salt who didn't love her garden more than any mortal soul.)

Well, she busted out of the door shouting at this half-grown hog in her compost heap. He'd been trampling down the pumpkin vines, so she put a curse on him that turned his tail straight. He staggered off and Sal thought she'd seen the last of him, but the very next day he was rooting off in the compost again.

She put a curse on him that time that turned his ears inside out. He staggered off again, his hooves going opposite directions, and took down one of the bean teepees in the process. Sal wanted to scream, but you can't stop pigs being pigs, so she grabbed her broom and shooed him out by the garden gate.

"Get gone!" she yelled. "You come back, I'll haul you down to the butcher and you'll be a raw head and bones by nightfall!"

Third day, she comes out on the porch and there Rawhead is, in the compost heap, with his tail straight, his ears inside out, and a rotten tomato sliding down his chin.

"You don't learn, do you?" says Sal.

*No, ma'am,* says Rawhead, and takes another bite of tomato.

You would have had to be a witch to hear him, but it's not all that surprising. Pigs aren't that far off from talking, most of them, and it doesn't take more than a few wishing melons to tip them right over the edge.

Well, things that talk are people, however they look, and you don't throw people out of the garden without offering them some hospitality. She invited Rawhead up to the porch and gave him a bucket full of water and yesterday's leftovers, and he sat next to her rocker and thumped his straight tail on the boards.

"How's that taste, then?"

*Tastes good, ma'am.*

"I see your momma raised you to be respectful," said Sal, rocking.

*Have to be, ma'am. If you aren't, she rolls over on you and squashes you flat.*

"Huh!" Sal rocked harder. "Not a bad notion. Know a few people who could've used a good squashing back in the day."

*It does make you think before you speak, ma'am.* He rolled a beady little boar eye up at her. *You cook good cornbread, ma'am. Can I stay with you a little while?*

"Huh!" said Sal again, and after that, you couldn't have found a closer pair than Sal and Rawhead the hog.

People tend not to mess with a witch, but there's always some damn fool who sees a woman living alone and gets thoughts in his head.

The next time someone tried, he got a tusk in his behind and went off yelling.

So word went out that Sal had a razorback hog as her familiar, and that did nothing but good for her reputation.

Well, stories always grow in the telling. Before long, they were saying Rawhead could talk, and after that they said he walked upright and sat in a rocking chair, same as a person.

Couple of people said some other things, too, about Sal and Rawhead, but there are people who say any damn thing.

The truth of the matter, as near as I ever learned it, was that Sal went on and Rawhead went on, and two days out of three, he slept on the porch at her feet and ate her leftovers. A razorback hog is a good friend to have in zucchini season, when the vines get huge and start throwing out zucchinis as big as your thigh. Useful for cleaning up yellow cucumbers, too.

Now, the way I always heard it, Silas the hunter had been one of those men who came sniffing around Sal when she was living alone, and it was Rawhead who broke him of that habit. But I've also heard that he was one of those folk who come up and try to give you charity you don't want. There was a lot of that going on up there, and nobody gets mad like a do-gooder if you won't hold still and let 'em do good on you.

Maybe he had a bit of a fancy for Sal, not in a marrying way, but thinking that somebody plain and lonely ought to be grateful for any attention. Maybe he thought that having a witch be grateful would be worth some trouble, or maybe he thought that a witch as good as Sal had a box full of money around the place.

But maybe those are just ways to make the story tidy again. The hunter could have just been one of those people who thinks he owns anything that doesn't have somebody else's name stamped on it. Lord knows, there's enough of them around.

One way or the other, a day came along when Rawhead didn't show up, and then another day, and then Sal started to get worried.

It wasn't like Rawhead to go away for more than a day at a time. His territory was the mountaintop, and he didn't leave it often. But pigs are social, same as human people, and they like each other's company. So Sal let two days pass, then three, and then she heaved herself out of her rocking chair and said some words I won't repeat in company.

She rummaged in her pantry 'til she found a good saucer, then she laid it on the table and filled it up with water and a drop of ink. The ink melted into the water and turned it black, and she breathed a witch's breath onto it.

Then she tapped her nail on the water's surface, and it rang like a bell.

"Good," she said. "Good. Now, show me the front porch." (Never ask to see something important right off. Water's tricky, even with ink to gentle it.)

The water showed her the front porch, with the empty rocking chair and the faded mat by the door. A wren flew up to the railing and looked around for something, then flew away again when it didn't find it.

"Good," said Sal. "Now, show me the sheriff's daughter, who ran off with the horse-thief."

The water swirled—though the surface didn't change—and Sal was looking at a girl wearing a clean apron, with a light in her eyes.

"Huh!" said Sal, pleased. "Glad it came out all right for her. Now, show me that razorback friend of mine."

The water darkened.

Under the table, where the water couldn't see it, Sal clenched her fist.

Then the water got light again—just a little—

And there was Rawhead.

She knew him right away, even though he was lying dead with three other hogs, in the back of a wagon moving down the road. She knew him just fine, and when the driver turned his head, she knew him, too.

Sal jerked back from the table and the water boiled away into steam.

She sat there for a minute, breathing through her nose, then she stood up. She picked up the saucer, because it was a good saucer with a little ink stained on it, and she washed it up careful, because a lifetime's habits die hard.

Her head ached and her heart ached, but she folded up the dish towel and set it back on its loop. She would have cried, but she didn't dare start.

"Somebody killed him," she said out loud. It felt like a knife, and she stabbed herself with it again—"Somebody went and killed my Rawhead."

That was better. If she said *Rawhead's dead*, she was going to fold right up like a broken leaf, but if she said *Somebody killed him*—well, then, that Somebody was going to have to pay.

The core of being a witch is that you don't fall down while there's work to be done. Sometimes that means you invent work to keep yourself standing upright.

She went to the coffee can in her bedroom and took it down. There was eighty-seven dollars stuffed into it, and Sal took the money out. It was all she had, and not a bad amount, but she didn't think she'd need it much longer.

Sal's nearest neighbor was a woman named Madeline, who had a hard life and stayed cheerful for it. People like that are a blessing and occasionally an affliction.

Even Madeline was a little surprised when Sal showed up while she was hanging out laundry on the line. She pinned up a sheet and turned around, and there was Sal, not five feet away.

Madeline yelped. "Lord, Sal, you about scared the life out of me!"

"Right," said Sal. "Came about the chickens."

Madeline wasn't quite done yet. "Seeing you right there like that! My heart's pounding, so it is. Let me sit down a minute. You can kill a body if you scare 'em too hard, you know."

"Don't have much time," said Sal bluntly. "It's my chickens. I'd appreciate it if you'd look in on 'em tonight and make sure they're in and fed."

"Sure, Sal," said Madeline. And then, though it wasn't the sort of thing to say to a witch, "You all right, hon? You're looking hard."

"Hard times," said Sal. "Take care of my chickens. If I don't come back by tomorrow, they're all yours. Watch for the rooster, he's a devil."

She turned away.

Madeline, moved by some spirit, called "You be careful, Sal!" and Sal's shoulder twitched, but she didn't make any reply.

She walked into town without talking to anybody. She watched for a certain wagon out of the corner of her eye, but she didn't see it, and she was glad.

"I'll fix him," she muttered. "I'll fix him good for this. But I got to figure out a way."

That's the real problem being a good witch all your life. Time comes when you need to do something real bad, and you don't have the knack for it. If she'd seen the man who murdered Rawhead walking down the street, what would she do?

She didn't have the sort of magic that made people drop dead. Hardly anybody did.

"I'd yell at him like a crazy old woman," muttered Sal, "and that'd be the end of me. Just some senile old woman yelling in the street."

But the wagon wasn't there, and she was still a witch.

So she walked on south for an hour, into the sandhills, looking for Elizabeth Gray.

Sal found her sitting on the front porch, looking over the sundew pool. Sundews are little devil plants, covered in sticky hairs, and when a bug lands on them, the sundew sticks it tight and eats it from the inside out.

Elizabeth Gray found their company congenial.

Sal came up on the porch with her heart in her eyes, and there were two chairs there, and a second cup of tea set out.

"Have a seat," said Elizabeth Gray.

Neither one of them saw fit to comment on the fact that Sal had been expected. They were both witches, and they knew how things were done. Sal took a sip of her tea and it was still hot, like it had just been poured a moment before.

She let out her breath, and her throat ached from not crying.

"Got a problem, I see," said Elizabeth Gray.

"It's my hog," said Sal. "My friend. That hunter shot him—Paul Silas did it, and he knows full well that was my Rawhead."

"Silas," said Elizabeth Gray thoughtfully. "Didn't his mother come from over by Bynum?"

"That's him. She wasn't a bad woman." Sal took another slug of tea. "Good thing she's dead. No mother ought to see what I aim to do to him."

Elizabeth grinned. "Listen to you," she said. "A white witch and all. What are you planning?"

"Don't know," said Sal honestly. "Had a thought, that's all."

And then she took a deep breath and said the words that witches hate to say, even to each other. "Need your help."

The porch creaked as Elizabeth rocked in her chair. Down by the sundew pool, the plants rippled.

"What's in it for me?" she asked. "That I ought to help you, who never did give me the time of day?"

"That ain't fair," said Sal. "You had your spot and I had mine. You ever asked, I'd have come. You know that."

Elizabeth Gray knew it, even if she didn't like to admit it. She tilted her head one way and another, and her neck bones popped and creaked like an old man's knuckles. "It's so. And you're in my spot now."

"I've got eighty-seven dollars," said Sal, and laid it out on the table between the teacups.

"You should've said," said Elizabeth Gray, all business. "Now, what is it you're looking to do?"

Sal told her.

The sun moved a little bit in the sky before anyone spoke again.

"Listen," said Elizabeth Gray, "listen close. You're asking me to bring him back, and I can't do that. Nobody can. You walk through that door and there's no walking back through. You know that, Sal, you're a witch to your teeth. You ever hear of anybody coming back for good?"

Sal stared into her empty teacup. "Thought you might have," she said quietly. "Figured maybe there was a way."

Elizabeth Gray shook her head, and that was truth, because witches don't lie to each other.

Sal stood up. She went down the steps and made three paces.

Then she sank down by the pool filled with sundews and put her bony hands over her face, because her friend was dead.

Elizabeth Gray's face didn't change. Her heart was still like sand and triumph ran through and pity ran through and neither one sank in.

But things do grow on sand, complicated things like sundews, and something grew now in the witch's heart that I wouldn't try to put a name to.

"I can't bring him back," said Elizabeth Gray. "But if you're willing, I can open the door."

Sal looked up, her face streaked with an old woman's tears.

"It'll take your life," said Gray, as if a witch's life wasn't any big thing. "Somebody's got to shove their foot in the door. He's all the way dead and you're all the way alive, and if you're willing, I can take you both halfway. I don't swear you won't wind up in one skin together, but it's the best I can do."

Sal thought about it. She thought about it hard, the way you do when every word in your head has an echo and you slam it down on the floor of your skull. She sat by the sundew pool and she thought, and Elizabeth Gray brought her another cup of tea, but all of it was second-guessing. She'd known what she was going to say as soon as Gray had made her offer.

"Do it," Sal said.

I'm not going to tell you what the spell was like. You think I want that sort of thing being common knowledge? You need a silver spoon to see by and a half-handful of rabbit tobacco, among other things, but that's as much as you're going to hear. Some stuff doesn't need to go any farther. You want to know details, go ask Elizabeth Gray.

She did the spell, anyhow. People say it was a hard spell, but I think that's because most people don't understand magic. It was easy, the way dying's easy or birthing's easy. It's not hard, it just hurts a whole hell of a lot.

Sal sat in the sand, because it was easier that way. Her hip joints ached getting her down, and she didn't think she'd be able to stand back up, but that didn't matter, because she figured she wouldn't be standing up again. Not in this life, anyhow.

The moon came up. It reflected in the pool, and Sal watched the sundews thrash and dance in a way that they don't do by daylight. Tiny little things they were, but they moved more like mice than plants, and they leaned toward Elizabeth Gray.

She was still watching the sundews when Elizabeth came up behind her with the big hog-killing knife and slit her throat from ear to ear.

Sal woke up with a scream and a gasp, in a body that wasn't hers.

She was hung upside down by her heels, and her whole body bucked when she moved and threw her sideways. It turned out to be a blessing, because she'd been hung up with a hook through her legs and she would have been hard pressed to free herself, but the convulsion knocked her right off the hook and onto the floor.

It was a fair bit of luck, witch's luck, but she was in no position to appreciate it.

It hurt.

It hurt more than anything ever had, more than she thought anything ever could. She'd been dead and now she was alive, and bodies don't much like that. When you're dead, all your muscles go limp, even the little ones that hold tense their entire lives. They didn't take kindly to being told to wake up and work again.

Her heart was the worst. Her heart tried to beat and there was stuff inside it that didn't want to move. It folded up like a fist around a knife blade and sprang open again.

Sal would have given her hope of heaven to stop that heart from beating, but the magic was in it now and wouldn't let it rest. It squeezed and opened, squeezed and opened, and inside the clotted heart, the blood broke up like ice on a river and began to flow again.

She had no idea how long she laid on the ground. It could have been hours. It felt like her entire life. But the dead body around her came back to life, slow as slow, and finally she opened her eyes and realized she was in the body of the dead razorback hog.

*Ma'am?* said a tiny little voice. *That you?*

If she'd been human, she would have cried, but hogs don't. She made a little whimpering squealing sound and scraped her trotters along the floorboards.

"Rawhead?" (It wasn't quite talking aloud, but he got the sense of it.)

*Yes, ma'am. What happened?*

"Think we've been dead, hon." Sal considered. "Well, you've been dead, and my body probably ain't alive if Elizabeth Gray did proper work with the knife."

She scrabbled her feet again, trying to get up.

*Let me,* said Rawhead, and the ungainly body was suddenly graceful, rolling to its feet and shaking all over.

"So that's the trick of it," said Sal. "Lord. Not used to being down here on four legs."

*It's easier than two.*

It did seem to be. Her vision wasn't so good, but things smelled strong, and the smells sort of worked with her eyes in a way she hadn't expected.

"We're in a barn, aren't we?"

*Think so, ma'am.* Rawhead turned in a circle and then looked up.

There were three dead hogs hanging from hooks overhead, their throats opened up to drain into a gutter in the floor. A fourth hook hung empty.

"Huh!" Sal stared at them. "Surprised there was any blood left in us. Must be the magic. I'll give her this, Elizabeth Gray's no slouch with the knife."

*Those three were my friends,* said Rawhead. *We ran around the mountain together.*

"I'm sorry," said Sal, suddenly shamed. "I didn't think. I'm sorry for your friends."

*It's all right. They'll go on. We all go on.* He dropped her—*their*—head, startling Sal again. *I'll miss them.*

There was nothing that a human could add to that eulogy. She didn't try.

The hog's body was huge and powerful. Sal tried moving it, walking unsteadily toward the door.

It was exhausting. It moved more or less as she asked—it worked better if she didn't concentrate too much on how the legs were moving—but the beating of their dead heart did nothing to revive her.

She got them around the corner of the barn. It was dim and noisy with crickets. She could smell turned earth and blood.

Their legs started to shake, and she had to sit down.

*This was madness,* she thought, trying to keep her thoughts away from Rawhead and not sure if she was succeeding. *I've trapped us both in this dead body, and for what? Revenge?*

*A witch should have known better. Now what? Even if I kill that bastard hunter, what then? Lay down and rot until there's not enough left of the body to hold us here?*

It was not a pleasant thought. Even less pleasant was the thought that the hog's body might rot away and their souls would be left chained to its bones.

Witches generally feel that there's plenty of work to be done here and now, but I never met one that wasn't secretly hoping to put their feet up for a while in the afterlife.

Now, though …

*Poor sort of friend I am. Silas only killed his body, but I may have made him into a ghost.*

*You're a good friend, ma'am,* said Rawhead staunchly. Sal realized that he'd been listening to her think the whole time. It would have been embarrassing if he was anybody else. She scuffled their trotters in the dirt.

"Did I hold you back from heaven, Rawhead?"

*Doesn't work like that for us, ma'am. We just go on to the next thing.*

"What's the next thing?" asked Sal. She was exhausted and felt like dying again.

*Oh, you know. We go around again. Think I was going to be a bird this time,* said Rawhead. *All curled up in an egg, with someone tap-tap-tapping on my shell. I like being a bird. It's good to fly.*

Sal wished that she could weep. Their mouth gaped open in distress. "What happened to that bird?"

*Won't hatch, I guess. It happens, ma'am. Don't worry.* It was hard to comfort herself in only one body. Hogs would normally go shoulder to shoulder, lean on one another, but with only one body between them, Rawhead had to settle for leaning against the barn wall and rubbing their jowls against their forelegs. *I don't mind coming back. We'll die again sooner or later, and I'll be a different bird.*

He paused and added generously, *You can come be a bird with me if you like, ma'am. I wouldn't mind.*

Humans are different from hogs in that kindness can break their hearts. Sal moaned through the dead razorback's throat.

"What the hell is that racket?" yelled a voice from inside the barn.

The boar's body jerked itself up and made a short bark of surprise before Sal quite realized what she was doing.

It was Paul Silas. Well, who else would it be?

"Damnit," she muttered, and "Damnit!" said Silas. She heard the distinctive sound of a gun being cocked. It was practically under her ear, on the other side of the wall.

Rawhead wisely took over at this point, backing them into the thicket of dog fennel and Queen Anne's lace that surrounded the barn. A beam of light came out of the barn, jangling crazily as the hunter carried the lantern. Sal saw the green gleam of spider eyes in the grass as the light moved over it, and a red flash from a whippoorwill blinking in the ditch.

"Who's there?" shouted Silas. "Who's sneaking around my—ah, god*damn!*"

"Found we were gone," said Sal silently.

Rawhead sank more deeply into the thicket. The light went flashing by, through the cracks between boards, and lit up the pebbles at the dead hog's feet.

Silas's footsteps paused by the empty hook, and then he walked to the mouth of the barn. The whippoorwill flew up and away into the trees.

"You a bear?" asked Silas. "You a bear out there, taking my meat? Or you a man?" He turned in a circle, and Sal saw the rifle outlined against the lantern light.

There's a whole story people tell when they're telling the story of Rawhead and Sal. It's a little bit like Little Red Riding Hood—the hunter says, "My, what big eyes you got!" And Rawhead supposedly says, "The better to see your grave." And the hunter says, "What a bushy tail you got." And Rawhead says, "The better to sweep your grave."

Well, a talking hog is one thing, but I never heard of a hog with a bushy tail. They say he took it off a dead raccoon, but if you can tell me why a boar would need a rotten raccoon tail to kill someone with, I'd dearly love to hear it.

No, what happened was that Silas stood in the circle of lantern light, holding his gun, looking for a bear or a thief, and Sal looked at him and heard his whining voice, and she remembered why she was mad.

That bastard killed Rawhead. He'd killed Rawhead's friends. In a roundabout way, he'd killed Sal herself.

And Sal remembered other things—the way Silas had treated a woman living alone, the way he'd come sniffing around like a dog after a bone, offering charity and more than charity, even when she'd made it clear she wasn't interested in the likes of him. She remembered a couple conversations on the porch that she'd rather not have had.

She thought of how those conversations might have gone if she'd been only a woman alone and not a witch. She remembered how they'd *almost* gone anyway, and a couple of nights spent with the door barred and her own rifle across her lap.

"I believe that man needs killing, Rawhead," she said.

*Yes, ma'am,* said Rawhead.

He moved.

The dead heart hammered in their chest, and Sal threw herself on the pain and took it all. When Rawhead charged, he was as quick on his hooves as a living razorback, and that is very quick indeed.

Silas heard the charge and turned. He got the gun halfway to his shoulder and fired.

The impact knocked the dead boar back a step—but only a step. He did not get time for another shot.

Their jaws closed over his thigh. Silas screamed, but not for very long. Humans die easy compared to hogs.

And then there was quiet.

After awhile the crickets started in again. The fireflies spread themselves out under the trees. The lantern guttered and went out.

Sal sighed. She felt ancient. The bullet in the dead boar's neck burned and she had no way to pick it out.

"Well," she said. "Well. I guess that's that."

*Yes, ma'am.*

The story that got around was a ghost story, so there's a proper ghost story end to it. They say Rawhead still rides around on the hunter's horse, and sometimes his head comes off and he holds it up to scare people with. They say he's still haunting these hills to this day, one more leftover thing from the old days, like the foundations you find in the woods sometimes, or the bits of barbed wire that turned up rusted in the fields.

But it wasn't like that, not in the end.

Sal and Rawhead walked. They walked clear back to her house, and that was a long and weary way. Rawhead heaved that dead body up on the porch for the last time and laid it down on the boards.

"Well," said Sal. She didn't have any regrets about Silas. She was so tired that regret couldn't get much foothold. It was more like a list in her head, checking off boxes—die, tick, take revenge, tick, come home, tick.

She felt like she was seeing the world from a long way away. Only Rawhead's voice was clear in her mind, as if he was standing right at her shoulder. "I … I don't know what to do now."

*Come with me*, suggested Rawhead. *We'll go be birds together.*

It sounded good to Sal.

They died again, on the porch. Rawhead knew the way. The dead heart, which had beaten so faithfully for so long, shuddered into stillness.

Madeline found the body the next day, and she knew enough about witches to cry over it. But Sal and Rawhead were long gone.

There's people who say that witches don't go to heaven. That sort of person acts like they're in charge of who goes in and out, though, and I don't know if God holds with that sort of thing. Maybe Sal did, maybe she didn't. It's not for me to say.

But me, I like to think that they found themselves curled up warm in an egg together, to sleep and dream of flying.

# THE DRYAD'S SHOE

*Author's Note: Tufted titmice are exclusively North American birds. The geography of Hannah's country is of questionable archetype.*

Once upon a time, in a land near and far away, there was a girl whose mother died when she was young.

Her mother had been merry and loving and devoted, but these things were no proof against fever. She died and was buried in a grave at the edge of the forest, past the garden gate.

In the way of young children, the girl (who was named Hannah) mourned for her mother and then forgot her. She visited the grave dutifully with her father, but her attention strayed more and more often to the garden fence, to the tall poles of beans and the thin green tentacles of the onions.

She loved the garden, which her mother had tended, and which was now under the care of an old man from the village. He showed her how to chit out fat nasturtium seeds and the importance of soaking peas before planting, how to prepare a bed with well-rotted leaves and break up the soil so that the plants could slip their slender roots inside it. He showed her how to keep a hive of bees without being stung too often—for a beehive was, in that time, considered a vital part of any garden—and when she *did* get stung, the gardener put dock leaves on it and patted her shoulder until the sniffles went away.

It was perhaps not a normal occupation for a young lady of moderate birth, but Hannah's father had little to say about it. He had little to say about anything since his wife had died. Hannah was ten years old before she realized that her friend's name was not simply "the Gardener," because her father never spoke to him.

The garden kept them well fed and Hannah was very proud on the days when the cook used *her* beets and *her* beans and *her* cucumbers to feed the household.

On her eleventh birthday, a bird flew down and landed atop a beanpole in front of her. The bird was gray above and white below, with a fine dark eye, no different than the other birds that flocked to the garden in the morning.

"Woe!" cried the bird. "Woe, child, what a state you've come to!"

*Your mother's dead,*
*Your hands are dirty,*
*Your father's away—*

Hannah picked up a clod of dirt and tossed it underhand at the bird, who dove out of the way.

It eyed her balefully, then settled back atop the beanpole, smoothing down its feathers.

"That wasn't very nice," said the bird.

"You started it," said Hannah. "It's not very polite to go around reminding people that their mothers are dead. And my hands are dirty because I've been thinning carrots, thank you *very* much."

The bird had the grace to look ashamed of itself. "It's the magic," it said. "It, um, comes over you. No offense was intended."

Hannah dusted off her hands. "I thought you might be magic," she said, "because you're talking, and birds don't, generally. But then I thought maybe you were a parrot, and I've heard that parrots can talk."

"I'm not a parrot," sighed the bird. "Don't I wish! Parrots are gloriously colored and they live halfway to forever. No, I'm only an enchanted titmouse, I'm afraid."

"I'm sure you're as good as any parrot," said Hannah, who was basically tender hearted toward animals when they weren't insulting her.

The titmouse preened a little. "Well," he said (Hannah was nearly sure that it was a he) "I *have* been enchanted. It's a great honor, if you're a bird."

"Who enchanted you?"

The titmouse stood on one foot and waved his other one toward the garden gate. "A mother's love," he said. "Also the tree just behind the grave, which is inhabited by a particularly sentimental dryad."

"Can you get seeds from a dryad tree?" asked Hannah, with professional interest.

"No," said the titmouse shortly. "They get annoyed if you ask. It's very personal for them."

"Oh, well." Hannah sat down on the edge of one of the beds. "What's it like to be enchanted?"

"It's marvelous," said the titmouse. "You're very focused all the time when you're a bird, you know. Here's a seed, there's a seed, this is my seed, give me back my seed." He fluffed up his feathers. "But when you're enchanted, all of a sudden you can see everything. Hello, independent cognition! It's a transcendent experience. Pity it doesn't last long."

Hannah had understood perhaps one word in three of that, but said politely, "It doesn't last?"

"No," said the bird sadly. "Only until my message is delivered. Would you mind? It's very important to the dryad."

"All right," said Hannah. "But no more making fun of my hands or talking about my mother."

"Mmm," said the bird.

"And no poetry!"

The bird lowered his crest a little. "Fine…fine…"

He gazed at the sky. Hannah went back to thinning carrots.

"All right," said the bird finally. "How's this? Your father's about to bring home a new wife."

"Yes?"

The titmouse paused, nonplussed. "You don't seem bothered."

"Well, it's not like *I* have to marry her. And the cook says it's about time he remarried and it does nobody good to keep moping about."

"Mmm," said the bird again. "You may find, I expect, that it's a little more tricky than that. Humans stay in the nest an awfully long time. But anyway. New wife, woe is you—she'll be unkind and treat you poorly."

Hannah scowled. "I'll put nettles in her bed."

"I can see," said the bird gravely, "that you are not without defenses. But should she treat you too abominably, you must go to the tree that grows behind your mother's grave and shed three tears and say—oh, this bit's poetry."

Hannah sighed. "All right, if you must."

The titmouse fluffed out his breast and sang:

*O chestnut tree, chestnut tree*
*Shake down what I need to me.*

Hannah gazed fixedly at the carrot seedlings.

"Dryads," said the titmouse apologetically. "They mean well, the poor dears, but they think if it's got a rhyme, it's high art."

"Well," said Hannah. "Thank you for the warning. I guess that will come in handy…"

"Glad to help," said the bird. "I'm sure we'll speak again. In factttcch *tchhh tchhirp!*"

He spread his wings, chirped again, like an ordinary bird, and flew away.

Hannah finished with the carrots and went to go ask the cook what the word *transcendent* meant.

Hannah's father did indeed come home with a new wife, and the new wife came with a pair of stepsisters, and things did not go as well as they could.

We will gloss over the various indignities, some of which are inevitable when households merge, some of which were particularly awful to this situation. Hannah's stepmother was tall and lean and beautiful and her daughters were tending in that direction. Hannah, who was short and sturdy from double-digging beds with shovels that were too large for her, was given a brief stare and dismissed out of hand.

"Poor thing!" said her stepmother. "Something should be done about the dirt under her nails, I suppose, but I am far too shattered from the move to take it in hand. I suppose she is not educated? No, of course not."

"I help out in the garden," said Hannah.

"Yes, I can tell by the dirt on your knees. Well, I suppose it keeps you out of trouble..."

Hannah went out into the garden, feeling very strange and rather as if she should be angry. It is not much use being angry when you are eleven years old, because a grown-up will always explain to you why you are wrong to feel that way and very likely you will have to apologize to someone for it, so Hannah sat on the edge of the raised bed and drummed her heels and thought fixedly about when the next sowing of beets would have to be planted.

After awhile, she scrubbed at her cheeks and went to go and plant them.

The next few years went along in that vein, more or less. Her stepmother did not wish to be bothered with her and her stepsisters did not understand gardening and Hannah did not understand embroidery or boys and so they had very little to talk about.

Her stepmother instituted a "no filthy nails at the table" policy, which meant that Hannah ate in the kitchen. It started as an act of rebellion against pumice stones and nail clippers, but eventually it just became the way things were. Hannah found it much more restful.

There was talk of sending Hannah to finishing school, but nothing came of it. The joy of getting rid of her was outweighed, to her stepmother's mind, by the exorbitant expense. So long as Hannah stayed out in the garden and made herself scarce, there was a minimum of trouble.

"It ain't right," muttered the cook. "She treats that girl like a serf."

The Gardener shrugged. "We're serfs," he said. "We do well enough."

"Yes, but she's not. Her father owns the house free and clear, not the Duke."

The Gardener was slow to reply, not because he was stupid but because he had come to a point where he considered his words very carefully.

After a time he said, "There are worse things. She's warm and fed. No one beats her."

"She should have pretty dresses," said the Cook, annoyed. "Like the other two do. Not go around like a servant."

The Gardener smiled. "Oh, sure, sure," he said. "Nothing wrong with pretty dresses. Do you think she could keep them out of the vegetable garden?"

The Cook scowled. Hannah's abuse of clothing was no secret. The laundry maids had to use their harshest soap on the knees of her trousers. What Hannah might do to muslin was not to be contemplated.

If anyone had asked Hannah herself, she would have shrugged. She had no particular interest in her stepmother or her stepsisters. The older stepsister was rude, the younger one kind, in a vague, hen-witted way, and obsessed with clothing. Neither understood about plants or dirt or bees, and were therefore, to Hannah's way of thinking, people of no particular consequence.

Hannah did not have any difficulty interacting with people; she just had little interest in doing so. She went to the village school long enough to learn to read, but never particularly embraced it, except insomuch as there were herbals and almanacs to be read. People in books tended to do very dramatic (or very holy) things and none of them, while trampling their enemies or falling in love or being overcome on the road to Damascus, ever stopped to notice what was growing along the sides of the road.

There had been an incident with the priest and the parable of the fig tree. Hannah had opinions about people who did not understand when figs were ripe, even if those people were divine. She was brought home in disgrace and her stepmother spent several days having vapors about the difficulties of an impious child.

In this not entirely satisfactory fashion, they bumped along until Hannah was seventeen and the Duke threw an extraordinary ball for his son.

"We are going to the ball!' said Hannah's older stepsister when Hannah came in with an armload of vegetable marrows.

"Good for you," said Hannah, dropping her armload on the Cook's table.

"You should come too," said the younger stepsister. "All the girls will be there. Everyone is wearing their very best dresses."

The older one snorted. "Fancy Hannah being there!"

"I hear the Duke has an orangery," said Hannah thoughtfully. She had never seen an orangery, although she'd heard of them. They were frightfully expensive and required a great deal of glass.

"An orangery," agreed the younger, knowing that Hannah was fond of plants. She chewed on her lower lip, wracking her brain. "And vast formal gardens with a hedge maze. And—oh, all manner of things! The centerpieces are supposed to be as large as wagon wheels, with so many flowers!"

"What would she wear?" demanded the eldest.

"Oh!" The younger stepsister considered. "We'd have to make her something. We could take in the hem on my green dress, perhaps—"

Hannah had not the least interest in floral centerpieces and only a vague professional curiosity about hedge mazes. She had less than no interest in hems and green dresses. But her stepsister meant well. She patted the other girl's arm and went back outside.

She also had no interest in the ball. Balls sounded deathly dull. It might have been a good excuse to enter the Duke's manor house, however, and perhaps there would have been tours of the orangery.

"But really," she said aloud, scowling in the direction of the beans, "it's probably not worth having to go to a ball. And she's right—what *would* I wear?"

"Ahem," said the tufted titmouse.

Hannah raised her eyebrows.

She was a good bit taller now than she had been at eleven, and so she and the bird were nearly at eye-level.

It looked like the same bird. Did they live that long?

Perhaps the magic ones did.

"I'm just saying," said the bird, "you haven't asked for anything. Not once."

"I did too," said Hannah. "I went and asked for a packet of nasturtium seeds. And received *nothing*, might I add."

The bird sighed. "Dryads do not deliver the seeds of *annuals,*" it said, with a good bit of contempt. "Anyway, you're not supposed to ask for anything. You're supposed to take what you're given."

"I would have, if she'd given me nasturtium seeds."

The titmouse rubbed a wing over its face.

"Just try it," it said. "Tomorrow night, when your sisters are gone to the ball."

"All right," said Hannah. "If it gets me a look at that orangery, I'll try it."

The titmouse turned its head from side to side, in order to give her the full effect of its disapproving stare. "An orangery."

"I want to see how it's done," said Hannah. "Oh, I can't build one, I know—I haven't the money for glass. Still, one might make do."

"You haven't got *any* money, have you?" said the titmouse.

"Yes, I do. I raise queen bees and sell them off. And I've been selling honey. The Gardener would normally take it but he hates going to the market. So I sell the honey for him and we split the money."

"Shouldn't the honey go to the house?" asked the titmouse.

Hannah shrugged. "It's not like we don't have plenty. And we're the ones who take care of the bees. "

"You're embezzling honey from your father," said the titmouse. "*Lovely.*"

Hannah had no idea what that word meant. "Um. Maybe? They're *my* queens, anyhow."

The titmouse clamped its beak shut and gazed at the sky in silence.

"Look, Silas at the market gives me a dollar per jar. And I get five dollars for a queen." Hannah was feeling a bit defensive about the matter.

"What do you *do* with that money?" asked the titmouse.

"Well, I buy seeds sometimes. Mostly I save it, though. It's all in a tin. I won't tell you where."

"Sound fiscal policy," said the titmouse wearily. "All right. Tomorrow night, don't forget."

"I won't," said Hannah, and the bird flew away.

It was a long morning. There was a great deal of uninteresting fretting about dresses. Hannah escaped into the garden as quickly as possible and set about thinning the carrots.

Even so, she caught occasional snippets through the windows—"Now remember, my dears, eye contact. You must make it boldly, but when he sees you, look down and blush. No, dear, that's a flush, it's not the same thing…"

And, a few minutes later, when the carrots were thinned, "*Positively* no drinking. Not even ratafia. Unless the Duke's son offers it to you, in which case you will allow yourself to be led by him. It is *vital* that you not become intoxicated."

Hannah moved on to the beets, thinking that it was all very stupid. It was hardly even worth planting beets, come to that, since it was starting to get hot and they were likely to bolt, but there was a wall of the house that got afternoon shade...

She lugged the watering can over to the shaded bed and encountered the Gardener.

"Going to the ball?" he asked.

"I doubt it," she said. "Though I hear the Duke has an orangery."

The Gardener snorted. "Lot of nonsense," he said. "You grow plants when *they* want to grow, not when you want them to."

"*You* use cold frames," said Hannah.

"Don't get smart," said the Gardener. Then he cracked a rare smile. "Ah, fine. I'd not have an orangery if you paid me—too many fiddly bits. But a little glasshouse for extending the season—well, perhaps."

Hannah grinned and went to plant beets.

Just before the supper hour, there was a great commotion and Hannah's stepmother and stepsisters poured out of the house in a froth of lace and seed-pearls. They climbed into a carriage (Hannah was secretly amazed that they could all fit) and drove off toward the Duke's manor.

"And not a word to her!" Cook groused to the Gardener. "Not a word! Her blood's as good as theirs."

The Gardener shrugged. "She's good with bees," he said. "Be a shame to waste her on a Duke."

The Cook stared at him as if he had lost his mind, but Hannah, who was pulling her gloves off, out of the Cook's sight, heard the praise and was warmed by it.

She ate her dinner quickly and went back into the garden. The back gate was overgrown, the hinges red with rust. She climbed over it instead of trying to open it, and landed with a thump in front of her mother's grave.

"Right," she said. "I'm here."

Nothing happened.

The wind sighed in the chestnut's branches. Hannah wiped her palms on her trousers.

Nothing continued to happen.

It occurred to her that she was standing on her mother's grave. That was awkward, but flinching away seemed even more awkward, so she had no idea what to do. She gazed up at the sky and said "Um."

The titmouse landed on a branch and looked at her. "You have to say the words," it said.

Hannah sighed. "Do I have to?"

"Yes."

"They're silly words."

The tree gave a long, disapproving groan, as if the branches were moving in a high gale. The titmouse fixed a warning glare on her.

Hannah took a deep breath and recited:

*O chestnut tree, chestnut tree*
*Shake down what I need to me.*

The leaves rustled.

Other than that, Hannah didn't see much difference.

"Um," she said after a moment. "Am I supposed to close my eyes, or do I go back inside and my problems are fixed, or…?"

The titmouse pointed one small gray foot over her shoulder.

Hannah turned.

Draped across the fence, looking absurdly out of place, lay a ball gown. It had enormous skirts that twinkled in the evening light. The sleeves were the color of a new leaf in springtime and belled out in enormous slashing ribbons.

"Good lord!" said Hannah, quite astonished.

"Now you can go to the ball!" crowed the titmouse.

"Um," said Hannah. "Y-e-e-e-s. That is a thing I can do. I suppose."

She glanced over her shoulder at the tree and the grave.

The bird beamed as encouragingly as something with a small, immobile beak can beam.

"Right," said Hannah. She gathered up the dress. There were gloves and shoes as well, and a neat black domino mask to hide her face. Her fingers slithered over the fabric, feeling the calluses on her fingertips snag at every thread. She winced. "Okay. Yes."

She slung the dress over her shoulder, climbed over the gate again, and went into the house.

The chestnut tree and the bird sat together in the growing dark.

"She'll be fine," said the bird. "I'm sure of it."

Late that night, the stepsisters returned. They were tired and downtrodden, and the youngest was carrying her shoes.

"A lady doesn't go barefoot," her mother said reprovingly.

"A lady doesn't have blisters the size of grapes then."

"Who was that girl?" asked the oldest, annoyed. "The one who came in late? The Duke's son didn't so much as glance at the rest of us after she showed up."

"I don't know," said her mother. "No better than she should be, I imagine!"

"I wish I had a dress like that," said the youngest wistfully. "No wonder he danced with her. I'd have danced with her too, in a dress like that."

The bird was asleep with its head tucked under its wing, but the tree jostled the branch and woke it up.

"Eh? What?"

It cocked its head, listening. "Oh. I see. Good for her, then. All as it should be."

The tree creaked.

"I imagine there'll be another ball soon," said the bird. "And another gown. Was she supposed to bring that one back?"

*Creaaaaak...*

"Hmm."

The next morning was bright and glorious. Hannah slept late and came out to weed the turnips with her eyes dark and thoughtful.

"Well?" said the titmouse, lighting onto a rain gauge.

"It's a magnificent orangery," said Hannah. "They're heating it under the floors, that's the trick. The fire isn't allowed to go out. You'd need three or four servants to keep it all going, though." She sighed, gazing over the garden. "Not really practical in my situation."

"Bother the orangery!" said the bird. "What about the Duke's son?"

"What about him?"

"You danced with him all night, didn't you?"

"I did nothing of the sort!" said Hannah.

The titmouse blinked.

"But...a girl showed up late in a beautiful dress..." it said slowly. "And the Duke's son danced with her all night..."

"Good for her," said Hannah. "There were dozens of beautiful dresses there, I expect. Hope it was the servant girl, though."

"The servant girl?"

"Sure." Hannah straightened from her weeding. "The one I traded the dress to for a key to the orangery."

The titmouse shot a nervous glance over its shoulder at the chestnut tree. "Come over by the beehives," it said, "and tell me what you did."

"Not much to tell," said Hannah, following the bird obediently. The buzz of the hive made a gentle background to her words. "I met up with a servant girl over by the gardens. She was dead keen to go to the ball, and I had a magic dress, so I gave it to her. Fit like a glove, might I add—though she had to pad the toes on the shoes, they're a little too large. In return, she smuggled me into the orangery." She rubbed the back of her neck. "I hope it was her."

"Why didn't *you* go to the ball?" squawked the bird. "That was the *point!*"

Hannah rolled her eyes. "Don't be ridiculous. What would I do at a ball? A bunch of people standing around being snippy at each other and not talking about anything of any purpose. I caught a bit of it from the servants as I was passing through the manor. No *thank* you."

"There's dancing, though!"

"I don't dance," said Hannah shortly. "Dancing's not a thing you just pick up in a garden."

The titmouse paused. "Um…" It shifted from foot to foot. "You could sway gracefully? Like a tree?"

"No," said Hannah. "Just…*no.* That is not how dancing works."

"But you're supposed to charm the Duke's son!" said the bird, hopping up and down in its agitation.

"I don't see how. Unless he likes bees."

She picked up her hoe again. "Anyway, the orangery design did give me a few thoughts. If what the plants want is warm *roots,* we're doing this all wrong. I have to experiment with some seed trays on top of the bread ovens."

The bird gaped after her as she left.

After a moment it said, almost to itself, "I don't dare tell the dryad. Chirrrp!"

In the way of all good stories, there was another ball announced within the week. "So soon!" said Hannah's stepmother. "I cannot get dresses fitted so quickly! Still—this is your chance to charm him again, my dears."

"No strange girl is getting in my way!" vowed the eldest.

"I still wish I had that dress…" said the youngest wistfully. "Even just long enough to see how they sewed the sleeves. And my blisters haven't healed yet."

Hannah heard all of this because she was in the kitchen, checking her seed tray. The seeds atop the oven had sprouted twice as fast as the ones outside. "Warm dirt," she muttered. "How do I keep the dirt warm?" She fisted her hands in her hair, not caring that there was earth on them.

The titmouse was on her the moment she stepped outdoors. "Another ball," it said. "Here's your chance. You can go and charm the prince—"

"Duke's son."

"Yes, him. You can charm him with your—um—graceful swaying—"

Hannah heaved a sigh. "You're talking an awful lot for a temporarily enchanted bird."

"It's because I'm supposed to get you to the ball. I'm your fairy godbird. Apparently. Anyway, I'm getting used to it. Now, go to the tree after your sisters leave for the ball…"

Hannah sighed again. "I don't have the least interest in the Duke's son, you know."

"I'm sure when your eyes meet, it'll be magic."

"I doubt it."

The bird thought for a moment. "If you marry him, you'll inherit an orangery."

This gave Hannah pause. Her finger drifted to her lower lip. "Hmm…that's a thought…"

"And someone else can do the weeding for you," said the titmouse.

Hannah frowned. "Will they? But how will I know if they can be trusted? You have to be very careful with the ones with taproots, you know. And bindweed. You leave even a shred of bindweed in the ground and it's all over." She put her hands on her hips. "And come to think of it, are Duke's son's wives even allowed to garden? Don't they make you wear white gloves and do deportment or something?"

The titmouse was forced to admit its ignorance of the doings of nobility. "I don't know."

"I shall check," said Hannah forthrightly. "The servants will know. I'll ask that nice servant girl about it tonight."

"You will?" asked the bird.

"Yes. She's bound to talk to me. I'll give her another dress."

The dress this time was the color of a summer sky and the mask was dusted with tiny crystals. The titmouse kept its grave reservations to itself. The dryad creaked approval as Hannah picked the bodice off the fence and went into the house.

The stepsisters returned an hour after they left. Their mother had a grim set to her lips.

"Where is she *getting* those dresses?" demanded the eldest.

"I wish I knew," said the youngest. "I don't even want to wear it. I haven't the hips for the one she wore tonight. I just want to see how they fitted it together." She chewed on her lip.

Hannah returned an hour later, carrying a sack. She dropped it in the shed and went inside, then returned a few minutes later carrying a lamp.

The titmouse, resigned to its duty, landed in front of the shed and squeezed in through a knothole.

Hannah bent over the potting bench, spilling out her sack. It contained dozens of little lengths of stem, some with bits of dirt at the bottom, some severed with a sharp knife.

"Dare I ask?' said the titmouse.

"Cuttings," said Hannah. She pulled out jars. "Willow water, willow water…ah, there we go!"

"Cuttings," said the bird. "I might have known."

"I think I can get most of these to root," said Hannah. "The servant girl's mother is an assistant gardener. She let me have free run of the gardens. Had to do it by moonlight, so some of these aren't as clean as I'd like."

The bird's beak gaped in distress.

"*And* she gave me some nasturtium seeds," added Hannah.

"And the Duke's son?" the bird asked wearily.

"Useless," said Hannah. "I asked. Apparently if you're a Duchess, you don't garden. You sit around and tell other people to garden for you. What's the good of that?"

"Some people might like it."

"If other people are doing the gardening, it's not your garden. And they expect you to have heirs and such."

"That's the general way of things, yes."

"Not gonna happen," said Hannah, dunking a stem in water infused with willow chips. "And *don't* tell me I'll change my mind when I'm older."

"Wouldn't dream of it," said the titmouse. It devoted a few minutes to settling the feathers on one wing. "Well. This is a fine mess."

Hannah shrugged. "The servant girl's happy. Her name's Kara, by the way. She knows how to dance, too. Apparently they practice in the servant's hall. And she has quite good manners, which I don't, and she's soppy about the Duke's son. Let *her* marry him."

The bird was silent.

Hannah carefully shook out her seeds into various jars, and labeled them in her rough, scrawling hand.

"There's going to be a third dress," said the titmouse finally. "Dryads like things that come in threes."

"Poison ivy comes in threes."

"Magic's similar. You don't notice you've run into it, and then it itches you for weeks."

"Well, I don't have to go," said Hannah. "I've seen the orangery and I've got all the cuttings I'll ever need. And Kara's got two dresses. She can wear the first one again."

"You'll have to take the dress, though," warned the titmouse. "The dryad will get very upset otherwise."

"She's a tree," said Hannah. "What's she going to do, drop nuts on me?"

"For my sake?" asked the bird. "It's her magic in my head, you know."

"Oh!" Hannah looked contrite. "I'm sorry, bird, I didn't know. Of course I'll take the dress. I don't want her to take it out on you."

"She probably should," said the bird mournfully. "I've made a hash of things."

"No," said Hannah. "You've been very helpful. I've been glad to talk to you."

She held out her hand, and after a moment, the titmouse jumped onto her thumb. Its tiny feet scratched at her skin, and it seemed to weigh nothing at all.

The titmouse was an excellent prophet. Three days passed, and then another ball was announced. Hannah's stepmother threw her hands in the air in despair.

"No," said the youngest stepsister, with rare stubbornness. "I'm not going. My feet are completely raw. And he's only going to look at that one girl anyway."

"She can't possibly have a new dress this time," said Hannah's stepmother.

"Then there's even less reason to go," said the youngest and locked herself in her room.

She stayed there for three hours, until Hannah tapped on her door. "Psst! Anabel!"

"Hannah?" She opened the door a crack. "Are they gone?"

"Long gone," said Hannah cheerfully, "and I've got something you might like to see. Open the door, will you?"

Anabel opened the door, and there was her stepsister, with her arms full of fabric.

The youngest stepsister let out a long breath. "That's a dress like that girl wore! But—but that's not—you're not—" She looked up, her eyes suddenly wide. "But you're not her! She's got totally different colored hair—"

"Ugh, no," said Hannah. "What would I do at a ball? But I've been supplying the dresses. It's—well, it's complicated. But I thought you might want to look at this one."

They laid the dress out on the bed. Hannah fidgeted while Anabel went over the seams, inch by inch, making appreciative noises, like "Will you look at what they did here?" and "Goodness, that's very clever. I wouldn't have thought to do that..."

"All wasted on me, I'm afraid," said Hannah cheerfully. "Anyway, keep it hidden, will you? If your mother finds out, there'll be questions, and I'll deny everything."

Anabel nodded. "I will," she said, sounding much less vague. "I can make a pattern from this, I bet. Thank you, Hannah!"

And she flung her arms around her stepsister, heedless of the dirt on Hannah's knees.

"You're welcome," said Hannah. "What are sisters for, after all?"

Long after midnight, Hannah's stepmother came home with her oldest daughter. Her eyes were bright—not with triumph, but with gossip.

"You will not believe what happened!" she crowed when Anabel came down to meet them. "It was—oh my, what a thing! You missed it!"

Anabel put the kettle on. Hannah came from her small room by the back door. Hannah's stepmother was in far too good a humor to protest. A story like this needed to be shared with as many people as possible. She would have rousted the neighbors if it hadn't been nearly dawn.

"The girl came back," said Hannah's stepmother. "In the same dress she wore the first time—"

Hannah's younger stepsister handed her a mug of tea, and they shared a secret smile.

"Not that the Duke's son noticed," grumbled the older stepsister. "Boys never notice clothes unless your neckline is halfway to your waist."

"Don't be vulgar, dear," said her mother. "But yes, she was wearing the first dress. And they danced and then at midnight there was an unmasking—you know how it is with these costume balls, everybody knows who everybody is, but you have to do the unmasking—"

"And she's been slipping out beforehand, apparently, so she never did unmask—"

"But this time the Duke's son was watching her like a hawk, and she had to actually run away—"

"—but she left a shoe! A shoe on the ground!" finished the older stepsister triumphantly.

"And he's snatched it up and is guarding it like it was the crown jewels," said her mother. She grinned wickedly. "Never realized he was quite so into shoes, but the way he was caressing it—well, you wonder a bit."

"What do you wonder about?" asked Hannah, who had been silent up until now.

There was a pause. The atmosphere in the kitchen, which had been cozy, started to cool—but her stepmother thawed, mellowed by the hot tea and the gossip. "Feet," she said bluntly. "Some men like a lady's feet. More than the rest of the lady. Fancy shoes are as good as ball gowns to them."

Hannah blinked. Then she thought of her own large, stomping, mud-caked boots and relaxed. Surely there was no chance of such boots becoming objects of desire.

"Then I never had the least chance," said Anabel, sounding decidedly cheerful. "A man who is into feet is *not* going to be interested in my blisters."

Hannah took her cup of tea back to her room. She hoped Kara was all right. Of course the shoe would have come off—it was too large for her. Probably the cotton had come loose. Oh, dear.

She fell asleep wondering what the Duke's son was planning to do with the dryad's shoe.

Not long after breakfast, the question was answered. It was market day, and Hannah was delivering honey to Silas, when there was a commotion in the middle of the square.

"Hear ye, hear ye!" called a man in the Duke's livery. "Hear ye! By order of the Duke, all young ladies are ordered to gather at their homes, to await the Duke's pleasure!"

Heads snapped up all over the market. Silas muttered something about *droit de seigneur* and reached under his bench for a cudgel.

"We're not going back to those days!" cried the cheesemonger, who had three daughters.

"And the Duke couldn't get it up anyway!" shouted the herb-wife. "Although if he wants to try some of my teas—"

"No!" said the herald. "No, you didn't let me finish! It's not like that! Nobody's droiting anybody's seigneur! And he doesn't need any tea!"

"Guaranteed to put fire back in an old man's belly!" cried the herb-wife, sensing a marketing opportunity.

"The Duke's son is seeking a mysterious woman!"

"I've got three," said the cheesemonger, suddenly interested.

"A *specific* mysterious woman!"

"Nuts."

"All girls of marriageable age in the village are required to present their left foot to try on a shoe!"

There was dead silence in the market.

Silas leaned over and murmured, "I always thought there was something a little peculiar about the Duke's son…"

"I'm sure he's very nice," said Hannah weakly, and slipped away.

Word spread quickly through the village. It was garbled at first, but the details rapidly filtered out. The Duke's son was coming. He had a shoe. Everyone had to try it on. The girl whose foot fit the shoe was the one whom he would marry.

"Oh, hell," said Hannah, staring down at her mud-caked boots. She wiggled her toes grimly.

The shoe was going to fit. The shoe was *made* to fit. That meant she was going to marry a Duke's son, and that meant no more gardening and no more beekeeping and instead graceful swaying and the producing of heirs—

"No," said Hannah furiously. The bees swarmed around her, buzzing like a tiny army. "No. Bird! *Bird!*"

"Eh?" The tufted titmouse landed on the fence. "What?"

"The Duke's son is coming," said Hannah grimly. "With a shoe to try on. You have to go get Kara. She has to be here to try it on."

The titmouse opened its beak to argue.

Hannah leaned in close. Her large human eyes met the titmouse's own small, dark ones.

She glared.

"Right-o," said the bird. "The dryad won't like it—"

"I'll take an axe to the dryad if I have to marry a Duke."

"Kara, you say?" The bird saluted and winged away over the garden.

Hannah exhaled through her nose and settled in to wait.

The shoe, when finally presented at Hannah's household, was much the worse for wear.

It had stains on it. One embroidered rose flapped forlornly. It had been tried on several dozen times and was looking stretched and shapeless.

It was still far too small for Anabel, who took one look at it and began laughing. "Oh, no," she said. "I'd have to hack my toes off. Will you look at these blisters?"

She wiggled her bare toes. The Duke's herald averted his eyes. Hannah's stepmother put her hand on Anabel's shoulder and murmured, "Not in front of the Duke's son, dear."

Hannah lurked behind the shed, watching the road for Kara.

"She has to get here on time," muttered Hannah. "She *has* to. I *won't* marry him."

The oldest stepsister tried on the shoe to no avail. The embroidered rose dangled by a single thread.

"Sorry to have bothered you," said the herald, turning away.

"Hang on," said Anabel. "There's still Hannah."

"Hannah was not the mysterious girl," said her mother blightingly.

"She might be." Anabel set her jaw stubbornly. "She ought to get to try, anyway."

Her intentions were good, but Hannah could have stuffed her headfirst into a beehive when the whole Ducal procession proceeded into the garden.

"Not there!" she cried, jerking her eyes from the road. "Don't step there! That's where the poppies are sown, and you can't compress the soil, or—oh, *bother.*"

"It's 'Oh bother, *your lordship*,'" said the herald.

His lordship stepped off the poppies and looked contrite.

"If you could just try on this shoe," said the herald, looking at Hannah's muddy boots with contempt. "Then we'll get out of your flowerbeds."

"I'd rather not," said Hannah, eyeing the shoe. "It looks… used."

"Duke's orders," said the herald crisply.

Hannah sat down and began unlacing her boot as slowly as possible. Where *was* that titmouse?

She pulled the boot off. The Duke's son was chased by a bee and began waving his hands frantically.

"You'll only get stung if you do that," said Hannah, much annoyed. She would not marry him, that was all there was to it. She spread her toes in an effort to make her foot seem wider.

The herald extended the shoe.

Her toes slid inside. She flexed her foot, hard, and said "Look, it doesn't fit at all. Much too…err…"

There was a chirp and a whisper of wings on her shoulder.

The garden gate slammed open.

"Wait!" cried Kara. "Let me try that shoe!"

All eyes turned to her. Hannah took advantage of the pause to yank her foot out of the shoe and cram it back into her boot.

The Duke's son's head jerked up.

"That voice," he said. "*I know that voice!*"

He snatched the shoe away from the herald and dropped to his knees, heedless of the mud. "Kara? Is it you?"

"It is!" she said, and stuck her foot in the shoe.

It was much too big and hung like a rag around her foot. The Duke's son stared at it in dismay.

"It got stretched out," said Hannah hurriedly. "Because my feet are so big. Tore the stitches, I imagine. Or the seams, or whatever they are. It's definitely her. Ask her a question only she would know."

"What did I say to you, during the first dance?" asked the Duke's son.

Kara leaned forward and whispered something into his ear.

The Duke's son's face lit up and he flung the shoe aside.

A moment later, he had swept the servant girl up in his arms and was striding toward the gate, while she laughed aloud in delight. The herald squawked and ran after them.

Hannah let out a long sigh of relief.

"Could've been you," said the titmouse on her shoulder.

"God forbid," said Hannah. "All I want is my own garden and my own bees. And perhaps to work out a cheaper method of under-floor heating."

"I expect you may get that," said the titmouse. "At least the bit with your own garden. Providing dresses like that—well, you're practically her fairy godmother. I should expect a reward will find its way here eventually. Particularly if a small enchanted bird were to show up and sing about the benefits of gratitude."

Hannah grinned.

"Perhaps Anabel and I can set up together. She can sew dresses and I'll keep bees. There are worse fates."

"The dryad won't be happy," warned the bird.

"Sod the dryad." She thought for a minute. "What about you, though? Aren't you supposed to go back to being a regular bird?"

The bird shrugged. "Didn't get you married. I may be stuck like this for awhile, or until the dryad gets distracted."

"You don't sound too bothered."

"Once you get in the habit of thinking, it's hard to stop. Perhaps you could throw me a worm now and again."

"I'd be glad to," said Hannah, and the titmouse rubbed its small white cheek against her round pink one.

"That's all right, then," said the bird, and it was.

# LET PASS THE HORSES BLACK

*My friend Tamnonlinear passed away last year. She curated Tam-Lin stories. I wish I'd written this sooner, so she could have added it to her collection.*

*I wish a lot of things.*

"The horses will be black," she'd said. "The Queen will ride on those, with her greatest nobles around her."

Janet rubbed her hands down the sides of her jeans, wiping sweat from her palms, and watched the animals prance through the crossroads.

They were seven feet tall at the shoulder and their hocks were feathered with stormclouds. Their eyes blazed silver and their reins were made of braided briars. When the Queen tugged on their reins, blood flowed from their skin and from their riders' hands and neither seemed to notice.

One of them, passing close to Janet's hiding place, turned its head and snapped a passing bat out of the air. Janet could hear the crunch of tiny bones. The rider laughed and patted his steed's bloody neck.

When it walked on, she could see the hoofprints burned into the road, smoking in the twilight.

*Sure,* thought Janet. *Sure, yeah, the first thing you'd notice about* those *horses is the* color.

"You have to stay hidden," the little mouse-eared elf had said. She was smaller than Janet and her skin was gray, with a thousand lines running through them like the channels of tree bark. Janet touched the back of the elf's hand, very delicately, and the skin was smooth like polished wood, not like human skin.

The elf gazed at the shape their hands made, barely touching. Her eyes were the green of madrone leaves, newly emerged in spring.

"You have to stay hidden. If the Queen sees you, she'll catch you. And that will be very, very bad. It'll be a little safer when the brown horses pass, but don't come out."

"Why are you telling me this?" asked Janet.

The brown horses passed with the rest of the Fae Court among them. There were more of them than there had been black horses, by a great number, but at least they were not bleeding. Janet shifted in her hiding place. It was cold and damp, but that was only to be expected.

She'd dressed in clothes she was willing to die in. It seemed like there was a good chance of that happening. But then she had stepped out the door and it was already getting cold so she'd grabbed the first warm thing she found on top of the clean laundry and now she was going to her death in a sweatshirt that read: OREGON—TEN MILLION BANANA SLUGS CAN'T BE WRONG.

*Typical.*

The elf turned her hand over and closed her oddly-jointed fingers over Janet's. Her wrist lay against Janet's ringless finger.

"Because we're leaving. And I love this place."

Janet studied the odd, narrow face across from hers. She could feel a pulse through her fingers, though it did not feel like a heartbeat. It sank and thrummed and swirled like fiddle music in the elf-woman's veins. "Why leave, then?"

The elf made a restless gesture with her free hand. Her small mouse ears flicked to catch sounds that Janet could not hear. "The Queen has called the rade. The last rade of the fairies in this land. Some of us could stay behind the last time, because they would return."

She gave a small, unhappy smile. Her teeth were delicately pointed behind her lips. "We said we were preparing for the Queen's return, so that there would be a place for the court to stay when they returned. But this time, she won't take that excuse…"

The brown horses were made of wood. They came in a hundred shades of brown, from cypress gray-green to golden yellow poplar. Bark clung to some of them, where the manes and forelocks would be, and their tails were great swinging root clumps, still clotted with earth.

*Are they alive? Does the Queen just call them up and then root them whenever they're done traveling?*

Janet had a brief, dizzying vision of a fairy stable that was half forest, of horse-trees rooted in the ground by the feet and tails, waiting to be brought to life.

She craned her neck, looking at the palest of the horses. Was one of the riders Lyn?

No. They were fairies, elves, some of them almost human but most of them not even close. They had antlers or hooves or heads like birds. One rider was a cloud of amber moths, swirling more or less above the saddle. One rode side-saddle to accommodate a massive serpent's tail.

None of them had the face of her brother.

"He'll be with the white horses," said the elf-woman. "Your brother, I mean."

"I still can't believe the fairies took him," said Janet.

The elf-woman shook her head sadly. "The Queen fancies mortals sometimes. She takes them. The King does too, sometimes, but he mostly lets them go afterwards. The Queen keeps hers for decades."

"It's not that," said Janet wearily. "It's…it's any of this." God help her, until the elf-woman had come out of the madrone tree to talk to her, she thought Lyn had gotten arrested or robbed a convenience store or something.

*I should have been so lucky…*

Janet saw the mouse-eared elf at last. She rode a horse the slick red of madrone bark, with shaggy, peeling strips around the hooves. Her ears moved endlessly, as if listening for someone in the shadows, but she was staring down at her hands on the madrone-horse's reins.

*I'm here,* thought Janet, as hard as she could. *I made it.*

She didn't think elves could read thoughts, but she hoped somehow that the other woman knew.

"I'll tell him," said the elf-woman. "To ride on the outside if he can. There's a few of them, you know, the ones on the white horses. The humans that the Queen is taking with her." She grimaced. "She keeps them like pets. It's cruel."

"She seems cruel," said Janet.

The pulse, still against her fingers, swirled to a frightened crescendo. "Yes," said the elf, pulling her hand away. She tucked it against her body. "Yes. More than you know. She'll kill us if we don't come with her. The ones tied to a human family are the only ones with an excuse, and they'll lie low anyway, in case she forgets."

"Can't you lie low, too?"

The elf-woman shook her head. "She'd come for my trees."

There were eight white horses the color of milk. Janet half expected them to be unicorns, but they were only horses. They wore bridles and saddles like normal horses and their riders were the first humans that Janet had seen that night, since she looked in her mirror.

She saw Lyn among them at last. His skin was very pale, almost as white as the horse's hide, and he had the set lips of a boy at a funeral who is determined not to cry.

He had not been able to ride on the outside after all, but he was only one horse deep at last. Good enough. She'd manage.

She took a deep breath and jumped out of the shadow of the trees.

"You have to pull him off the horse," said the elf-woman. "You have to do it quickly. The Queen can't control mortal horses very well, but she can send them mad. If you get him off the horse before she knows what's happening, though, she won't bother."

She sat back. "After that...after that, it will be hard."

Janet ducked under the first white horse, grabbed the second one's bridle, and Lyn stared down at her with his mouth hanging open.

*"Janet?"* he said. "What are you doing here?"

"Trying to help," snapped Janet. She grabbed his ankle and yanked. The horse shied and Lyn (had he ever even been on a horse before?) slipped and squawked.

"Give me your hand!" she growled.

He got the message or else he was grabbing for something to hold onto. Either one worked. She caught his hand and half-dragged him out of the saddle.

The other white riders set up a cheer.

"Do it!" cried the one on the first horse. "Lady, hold him!"

They turned their horses and suddenly there was a ring of white around them, with Janet holding Lyn in the center.

"Stay strong!" cried another rider, an old man in ancient armor.

And then, in a voice like shattering bells, the Queen cried *"What is happening here?"*

"She'll turn him into beasts," said the mouse-eared elf. "A lion or a wolf or a bear. A few of them. You have to hold onto him through it all. If you let go, she wins."

"I have to hold onto a *bear?*" said Janet, horrified.

"Or a snake," said the elf-woman. "She's fond of snakes..."

It was a lion first. Janet saw her brother's face melt like candlewax, and his open mouth grew fangs as long as her thumb. She ducked her head down into its mane and wrapped her legs around the beast's belly thinking *this is it, this is where I die, no one is going to believe it...*

The lion roared in her ear and left her head ringing. He could not get at her with his teeth, but he sank his claws into her back and she felt the sweatshirt shred away in rags and her skin with it, and then he brought up a hind leg and scratched like a dog scratching and itch and his claws tore her leg open and she was going to bleed to death and they would find her body and think—what? A mountain lion? An escaped zoo animal?

"If you will not relinquish your grip, then try another!" shouted the Queen and the world changed.

Her sweatshirt was whole again. Her leg was no longer torn open. The circle of white riders was still there, and the old man in armor said "Well done!" and then Lyn turned into a bear.

It was so massive that her arms ached spanning its body. She grabbed handfuls of fur, trying to hold on. This time, the bear hugged her back.

Things snapped in her chest like tree branches. She knew that sensation, knew that her ribs were broken and if she breathed, the ends would jam into her lungs but that didn't matter because she couldn't breathe anyway, the bear was crushing the breath out of her and it smelled rank and terrible and wild.

*It doesn't matter. Hold on. Just hold on.*

Her hands were locked in the bear's fur. She focused every ounce of will on her fingers, feeling the strands slide loose one by one. *Hold on. Hold on.*

"Or this!" cried the Queen, and the bear dwindled away into a slick, muscular surface as thick around as her thigh.

Janet drew in a breath that didn't hurt and her ribs were no longer broken. Her breath came out in a huff of laughter, because what was this? This was only pain, and Janet knew too much already about pain.

The white riders heard her laugh and they shouted like spectators at a football game. Were they on her side? They sounded as if they were on her side.

*Some of them have been her pets for decades, the elf-woman said. Perhaps there was no one to come for them.*

The serpent hissed and tried to slither out of the circle of her arms. It was too slick to hold like she had the bear.

She grabbed for its head instead and it opened its mouth to strike.

*Unimaginative,* she thought grimly. *If the Queen had any wits, she'd turn him into a porcupine. Or a cactus.* But Janet had grown up moving snakes off the road before a car could hit them, and this part, at least, was easy.

She jammed her forearm into the snake's mouth and it clamped down.

The pain of the fangs was like daggers, but that didn't matter. That was only pain. She flung her other arm over the top of the snake's head and now it was trapped against her, unable to release its mouth. The long body lashed and the tail spasmed.

"I—will—not—let—go!" snarled Janet into the snake's forehead.

"Enough," said the Queen.

The pain in Janet's forearm ebbed away and she was sitting on the path with her brother Lyn clutched in her arms.

The circle of riders opened.

It seemed to Janet that they moved aside reluctantly, but move they did. The Queen, on her great black horse with silver eyes, came walking into the center of the circle.

She leaned forward over the horse's neck and looked down at Janet.

"Very well," she said. "Very well. You have pulled him down and held him. This I acknowledge."

Janet looked up into the face of the Queen of Fairies.

She was beautiful. She was beautiful like stars were beautiful or moons or photos of distant galaxies. There was nothing human in her face, nothing that Janet's eyes could catch onto. She had no idea, even after gazing for a long time, what the Queen looked like.

"What is he to you, then?" asked the Queen. "Your husband? Your lover?"

"My brother," said Janet. In her arms, Lyn was breathing in wet, heavy gasps, his eyes closed.

"You have earned your kinsman back, then," said the Queen. "I did not know he had a champion."

Slowly, slowly, Janet stood up. She had him by the hair, still, in case the Queen had a trick left to play.

She looked the Queen of Fairies full in her impossible face and said "He doesn't."

A moan went through the white riders, a sound like the wind through pine trees.

She had moaned like that when Lyn had broken her ribs when she was ten. That was when she had learned what it felt like to have branches break inside your chest.

She flexed the fingers of her free hand, the one that had lay across the elf-woman's palm. The last two fingers on that side would always be crooked, from the time where her brother had ground his heel into her hand.

That was when her mother had thrown Lyn out of the house. The first time.

Perhaps it would do him good to learn what it was like to be at the mercy of a greater power.

Janet looked past the ring of shaken white riders. Her eyes picked out a slender figure on a slick red horse, with mouse ears and eyes the color of new madrone leaves.

She set her foot on her tormenter's shoulder.

And she smiled a very human smile at the Queen of Fairies, and said "I'll trade you."

# THIS VOTE IS LEGALLY BINDING

*There was a stretch in 2016 where everybody and their brother had a hot take article on trying to talk to women wearing headphones. After about the third such thinkpiece, I was moved to poetry.*

Someone always says it, whenever it comes up:
"I guess I'm just not allowed to talk to anyone any more!"

Well.
Yes.
It is my duty to inform you that we took a vote
all us women
and determined that you are not allowed to talk to anyone
ever again.

This vote is legally binding.

Yes, of course, all women know each other,
the way you always suspected.
(Incidentally, so do Canadians. I'm just throwing that out there.)
We went into the women's room at the Applebee's on the corner of 54
and all the others streamed in through the doors
into that endless liminal space,
a chain of humans stretching backward

heavy skulled Neanderthal women laughing with New York socialites,
Lucille Ball hand in hand with the Taung child.
We sat around in the couches in the women's room
(I know you've always been suspicious of those couches)
and chatted with each other in the secret female language
that you always knew existed.
Somebody set up a console—
the Empress Wu is ruthless at Mario Kart
and Cleopatra never learned to lose
and a woman who ruled an empire that fell
when the Sea People came
and left no trace
can use the blue shell like a surgical instrument.

Eventually we took the vote.
You had three defenders:
your grandmother and your first-grade teacher
and an Albanian nun who believes the best of everybody.
Your mom abstained.
It was duly recorded in the secret notebooks
that have been kept under the couch in the Applebee's
since the beginning of recorded time.
And then we went back to playing Mario Kart
and Hoelun took off her bra
and we didn't think about you again
except that I had to carry this message.

So anyway
good luck with that
it's just as you always said it was.
Hush now,
no talking,

hush.

# TELLING THE BEES

*I grew up reading Cricket Magazine, with the little bug comics along the bottoms of the pages. This story was eventually reprinted in Cicada, their young adult magazine, and I danced around yelling, because it was Cricket and I hadn't known how much that would mean to me until it happened.*

*This is based on an actual superstition that bees must always be informed if the master of the house has died.*

There was a girl who died every morning, and it would not have been a problem except that she kept bees.

When her heart had shuddered back to life and she had clawed her way back from the lands beneath, she sat up and drew a long sucking breath into the silent caverns of her lungs. Her first breath was always very loud in the little cottage, but there was no one there to hear it.

She wrapped her robe around her. It was a dressing gown in the morning and winding sheet at night. Then she swung her feet over onto the floor and the cold tiles were no colder than the palms of the newly dead.

She stumped out to the beehives and tapped each one with the key to her cottage, three times each. "The old master is dead," she said, as the hives buzzed and the bees swirled around her. "I am the new master." And she said her name, three times each over every hive.

Sometimes a bee would land on her wrist and wiggle its antennae at her. Sometimes it wouldn't. There was a bit of blue embroidery on the collar of her dressing gown, and the bees had to investigate it thoroughly some mornings, while other mornings they ignored it entirely.

When the hives had been advised of her passing, she went back into her cottage. Her feet left dark tracks in the silver grass. She made tea and ate honey scraped over black bread. That was all she ever ate. She had given the garden over to flowers, because it is hard for the dead to eat parsnips. The bees liked the flowers, and the bees were her best company.

She did not mind the bread, if there was honey. And even the dead will drink tea if they can.

She worked all day, weeding the garden and patching the cottage and tending the bees, and then at night, because she did not sleep, she would stay awake and watch the stars. They were old friends now, the bright beads of Orion and the Great Bear. They turned and turned about, as the seasons changed, but like her, they were always fundamentally the same.

There were no constellations that represented bees. This was a grave oversight. She had mentioned it to those in the lands beneath, but they looked at her with their gray faces and their sewn-shut mouths and few of them could remember things like "bees" or "stars."

Possibly she was not dead long enough. If she had stayed dead for more than a few hours, perhaps she could have found someone with authority. A person who understood about bees might understand other important things.

Slightly before dawn each day, she died.

Sleep like death and death like sleep are common curses. It is inevitable that they become tangled. Fair folk and wicked queens are not always precise in their diction.

There are consequences for imprecision, and it is always someone else who has to pay.

The important thing is not to dwell on it.

The bees had to be told, though. Bees are conscious of their dignity, and if you do not tell them of a death, they will stream away from the hive in a thrumming ribbon, going away, away, to someone who will respect them. It does not matter that the name of the living may be the name of the dead. They must be told.

It had been a long winter of dry black bread before she learned, with only the stars and the dead for company. She preferred the living hives and then, when the queens slept, the memory of wings and sweetness.

Surely there was a place where the bees went, under the earth. She had begun to look for them in the hours of her death, for the dead queens arrayed in black and gold. Sometimes when she woke, before her first breath, she could hear their buzzing and thought *I am getting closer.*

Surely they would help her, if only she could find them.

Even if it meant getting up now, every morning, with her blood still oozing sluggish in the chambers of her heart, and walking through the meadow with the house key in her hand, to go and tell the bees her name.

# THE TOMATO THIEF

Grandma Harken lived on the edge of town, in a house with its back to the desert.

Some people said that she lived out there because she liked her privacy, and some said that it was because she did black magic in secret. Some said that she just didn't care for other people, and they were probably the closest to the truth.

When her daughter Eva asked her to move into town, to be a little closer, Grandma Harken refused. It got to be a regular ritual with them—"Mother, won't you move in a little closer? I worry about you out there alone."

"What's going to bother me out here?"

"You could step on a rattlesnake," said Eva.

"I'd rather get bit by a rattlesnake than the neighbors," said Grandma Harken. "I get enough people coming whining to me as it is. As it is, some of 'em get tired and turn around. A twenty minute walk has its advantages." She held up a needle and threaded it on the first try. "Besides, I can still see what I'm doing. Talk to me when I've gone blind."

Eva sighed, the way she always did, and said, "If you won't come in closer, you could have someone come out and live with you. Hire a girl, maybe."

"Garden only feeds one," said Grandma, which was at least three-quarters of a lie. Eva knew this, but didn't possess the sort of steel that would allow her to call her mother out on it.

"You could at least get a dog."

"Can't get a dog. It'll offend Spook-cat."

(Spook-cat was a tiny ginger tomcat who lived in perpetual terror of loud noises, sudden movements, and unexpected shadows. He lived under Grandma Harken's bed and would occasionally consent to sleep on her pillow, despite her snoring. He was deeply intimidated by the jackrabbits that lived in the desert, so trips outside to do his business lasted less than two minutes, followed by immediate retreat back under the bed.

He had seen a mouse once and it had frightened him so badly that he had not come out from behind the stove for a week.)

Eva sighed again.

It was debatable whether she knew the real reason that Grandma Harken lived so far out of town. Her mother kept a lot of secrets.

In fact, it was because of the tomatoes.

Tomatoes are thirsty plants and they don't always want to grow in a desert. You have to give them criminal amounts of water and they'll only set fruit in spring and autumn. Summer heat is too much for them and if they don't die outright, you're pouring gallons of water a day into the sand just to keep them alive.

Grandma Harken had spent the better part of fifty years growing tomatoes and she had a spot in her garden that held water just a fraction longer than anywhere else. It got shade in the worst of the afternoon and sun in the earliest part of the morning.

Her tomatoes were the biggest and the juiciest in town. She started them on the windowsill on New Year's Day and she planted them out in February. They ripened in spring and she pulled the plants up as soon as the last one had been picked.

The same people in town who muttered about black magic swore that she was using unholy powers on her tomatoes. This was a little more plausible than general black magic, because obviously if you *had* unholy powers, you'd want to use them on your tomatoes. But Grandma Harken was extremely useful to have around and knew more about dangerous desert spirits than anyone else, so people shushed their whispering neighbors and smiled politely when Grandma passed.

Also, if you were very polite, you might be able to beg a few tomato seeds from her. The resulting plant wouldn't be up to her standards, but it would still bear a damn fine tomato.

Grandma Harken had been watching her tomatoes very closely for the last few days, and not just to catch the hornworm caterpillars.

One of the smaller ones was starting to come ripe, and she was looking forward to it more than a little.

She'd been feeling worn out and overly responsible lately. It had been a long, long year, and there'd been that business with her grandson and the jackalope wife. It had all worked out as well as could be expected, but it had been a worrisome mess while it lasted. Her grandson had gone back east on the train, and good riddance to him. Boy had no business in the desert. But she worried anyway, partly for him and partly for his mother and partly because a foolish young man with brooding eyes can cause no end of heartbreak in the world.

Worrying didn't do any good, but somehow that never stops anybody. Mostly it made her tired.

She didn't *look* any older, so far as she could tell from the mirror, but her heart felt like somebody had been scraping the last bits out with a spoon.

If she could just sit down at the table with a knife and salt and some good white bread, maybe a little mayonnaise ... well, it seemed like that'd put the world back into the right sort of shape around her. Sometimes the best cure for life was a ripe tomato.

She got up the morning after Eva visited and went out to the garden. The air was still cool and the porch steps creaked as she walked down them.

The tomato was gone.

Grandma Harken knew right away that it was missing, but she looked around the plants anyway. There were three of them, planted in a triangle, covered in heavy green balls. A few were turning red, but the tomato she'd kept her eye on, the one that had been right *there* ...

Gone.

It had been there last night. She'd looked at it in sunset and thought that it'd be ripe this morning.

"I ain't losing my mind," she said firmly. "That tomato was *here.*"

The tomato continued to be absent. There were no seeds on the ground or tracks in the dirt to indicate where it had gone.

The rest of the garden was large and dusty, like desert gardens often are. Jackrabbits liked to come lie in the shade under the beans. Jackrabbits aren't known for eating tomatoes off the vine.

Strange things happen in the desert. Grandma Harken looked around suspiciously and went back inside to make tea.

Two days later, there were two fine tomatoes almost ready to split. Grandma Harken stroked their scarlet skins. "Tomorrow," she said, with satisfaction. She had almost succeeded in putting the previous tomato out of her mind.

But tomorrow came and Grandma Harken beheld a distinct absence of ripe tomatoes.

This time she went over the garden practically on her hands and knees, but she could not figure out where the tomatoes might have gone. Jackrabbits didn't steal tomatoes, and javelinas, which might, would have made a fine mess of the garden. It was too high up for a box turtle, unless somebody was outfitting box turtles with stepladders these days.

"It ain't a kid from in town," she muttered. "They know better than to try, and anyway there's no footprints." The only marks on the dusty ground were from Grandma Harken's own sandals.

She prowled around the edge of the garden and found nothing. The fence was undisturbed.

She was crouched in front of the plants, staring at them, when she saw it.

She breathed in sharply. It was easy to miss, but if she looked in exactly the right place, she could see what looked like a single human footprint in the dirt between the three tomato plants.

She was so still for so long that Spook-cat came up and twined around her, making small *mrrrrp?* noises. She rubbed him under the chin automatically, barely noticing.

A thrasher called from the palo verde at the end of the garden. The noise sent Spook-cat skittering inside, and woke Grandma from her reverie.

The footprint had five clear toes. The owner had been barefoot.

"*Thief,*" hissed Grandma Harken, and stomped back indoors in a bitter state of mind.

She wrapped herself up in a quilt that night and sat in the rocking chair on the back porch. "We'll see what kind of rat bastard steals an old lady's tomatoes," she grumbled.

(Grandma Harken thought of herself as an old lady, because she was one. That she was tougher than tree roots and barbed wire did not matter. You did not steal an old lady's tomatoes. It was rude, and also, she would destroy you.)

She leaned her shotgun up against the porch railing in easy reach. Probably she wouldn't need it, but there was no telling how low a body would sink once they'd started down the road of tomato theft. Murder was not out of the question.

*Though I'll try to aim for the legs,* she thought, and grinned fiercely to herself.

The sun sank and the sky blazed redder than a ripe tomato. The herb leaves rustled and the bean plants whispered to each other farther down in the garden. The great sprawling squash had not yet set fruit, but they were sending questioning tendrils out in all directions, and the peppers were the size of Grandma's thumb. All around her, the garden whispered, a slow exhale after the heat of the day.

Grandma Harken leaned back in the rocking chair and fixed her eyes on her tomatoes.

She woke in the morning with dew collecting on the quilt. Her back was stiff and two more tomatoes were missing.

She shot out of the rocking chair fast enough to knock it over on its runners and cussed the air briefly blue.

"Jesus, Mary, and Joseph!" she said, when she'd run out of swear words and turned back to religion. "This ain't funny anymore!"

She stomped down and found a nearly ripe tomato, which she yanked off the vine and took inside. It sat on the counter. A day or two and it would be almost as good as the others.

Almost.

She was angry now at herself as well as the thief. Falling asleep when she was supposed to be standing guard—what was *that?* Was she really that doddering an old woman?

"Not tonight," she said grimly. "Not tonight."

She watered the garden by hand and did the laundry, just to keep herself moving. She napped all afternoon, which Spook-cat quite enjoyed.

Then, as evening fell, she brewed herself up a pot of cowboy coffee, with the grounds still in the pot.

It cost more than blood these days, but that was life. Salt, flour, coffee, and sugar were the only things Grandma Harken bought at the store, and the store could only get them in because Father Gutierrez was on good terms with the train-priests.

It didn't matter how good the terms you were on, though, they were expensive as the devil. Most of the time she got by with tea and honey and cornmeal, same as everybody else.

Still, didn't matter how strong you brewed it, tea was no substitute for coffee.

"I'll be up half the night drinking and the other half peeing," she said. "Not a chance I'll fall asleep this time."

She sat down in the rocking chair with the coffee mug in one hand and prepared to wait.

In the small hours of the night, Grandma Harken woke up because her bladder was killing her.

Her first thought was that she'd fallen asleep again, and damnit, she wasn't *that* old.

Her second was that the thief was less than ten feet away.

It was a mockingbird.

Grandma Harken stared.

It glowed like silver under the moon—really glowed, every feather edged in white fire. When it shifted, it threw light across the prickly tomato leaves and left sharp-edged shadows across the ground.

The bird perched on top of the tomato cage for nearly a minute. Occasionally it would flick its tail and set the shadows dancing.

It might have sat there all night, except that Grandma Harken's bladder was making its displeasure known. She squirmed in her chair and the rockers creaked on the porch.

The white patches on the mockingbird's wings blazed up and it flew.

She shot out of her chair, bladder be damned, and charged down the steps. She could see the mockingbird flying, the sagebrush casting fantastic shadows, the saguaros briefly silver instead of black—and then it was a distant spark dwindling into the desert.

Grandma Harken watched it vanish against the sky.

"Mockingbirds," she said aloud, stomping toward the outhouse. "Mockingbirds stealing my damn tomatoes."

She knew mockingbirds eat fruit if they can get it, but she had to admit, she would not have expected one to make off with a full-sized tomato. *Cherry or grape tomatoes, sure, but one of my big ones?*

She was up and down three more times that night, as the cowboy coffee made itself felt, but she was hardly sleeping anyway.

Mockingbirds also don't leave human footprints. And generally they do not glow like foxfire.

"Shapechanger," she said to Spook-cat, who slept in a small orange puddle atop the pillow. "Jesus, Mary, and Joseph. *Again.*"

The next night, she didn't bother with coffee. She cleaned up the house and shooed Eva off when she looked inclined to stay late.

"I don't need you fussing over me," she told her daughter. "I ain't gonna change and it's just gonna make us both snappish."

Eva was weak-eyed, mild-mannered, and had a disposition as yielding as a featherbed. It was hard to imagine her being snappish about anything.

But she'd also known her mother for a very long time, and she recognized *make us both snappish* as an olive branch. She stood looking down at the dishcloth in her hands, and said finally, "I'm worried about Brandon, that's all."

"He's back east," said Grandma Harken. "With your father's kin. He'll be fine."

"Do you think so?" asked Eva.

Grandma Harken was sharpening her garden shears. Her hands slowed on the file and she said finally, "He'll get in trouble and he'll figure it out. Best to do it without us standing over him. It's the only way anybody ever learns to clean up after themselves."

"He's been so upset since the girl—"

Grandma Harken threw down the shears. "He did a damn fool thing, and I cleaned up the mess for him. He *should* be upset. I'd be more afraid if he wasn't."

She exhaled and picked up the shears again. There was a burr in the edge of one blade and she set to work on it with the file. "Not your fault," she said. "I shouldn't yell. But see what I mean? I'm not fit for company now."

Eva looked at her.

"I ain't been sleeping well." Grandma held that out like a peace offering, because her daughter was sweet, not stupid.

Eva nodded. She threaded the dishtowel through the ring by the little sink. "Can I do anything?" she asked.

"Let me stew in my own juices for a day or two," said Grandma Harken. "Go fuss over someone who'll appreciate it."

Eva smiled faintly. "You're the one I worry about."

"I'm not dead yet," said her mother. "And I've still got a trick or two left to play."

She made an effort to be pleasant for the rest of the evening, and even let Eva extract a promise that she'd try to sleep more.

*It ain't a lie exactly. I'll try to sleep more once I've stood off my tomato thief. Whatever they might be under the feathers.*

As soon as her daughter had left, her whole demeanor changed. She laced on her good boots, in case she had to run, and locked Spook-cat in the bedroom. She put her garden shears in her apron pocket and made sure that her shotgun was loaded up with rock salt.

Grandma Harken knew more about shapechangers than anyone in town would have guessed, and that meant that she knew enough to be careful.

*Mockingbirds are cousins to ravens, and that's a bad game to get mixed up in. Never had any patience for riddles.*

"Blessed St. Anthony," she prayed, as she folded her quilt, "give me strength to defend my tomatoes."

This seemed like a rather trivial thing to bother a saint with, once she said it aloud, so she added "And—err—defend me from temptation, amen."

She pulled out her silverware drawer and dumped it on the kitchen table. With a ball of twine in one hand, she set to work.

By the time night fell, her best kitchen chair had been altered all out of recognition. She'd tied every fork and spoon to the back of it, flat with the bowl up or the tines out. Leaning back onto it would get you poked in a dozen places. There was one ladle aimed directly at the small of the back.

Grandma Harken was rather proud of that ladle.

She dragged the chair out on the porch and sat down on it, sitting bolt upright. She had a cup of tea in one hand—herbal, because she didn't need to spend another night like the last one.

And she waited.

She dozed off once or twice, but as soon as she slumped backwards, the forks and the spoons jabbed her awake. The moon moved carefully in the sky overhead.

It was nearly midnight when she fell asleep—really asleep—and that lasted nearly a minute. But the ladle prodded her in the small of the back and forks were pressing into her shoulder blades and she came awake immediately.

The mockingbird landed atop the tomato cages and looked around. It was impossible to read anything in those small white eyes, but Grandma Harken thought it looked … furtive.

She kept her eyes lidded. Surely the porch was too dark for it to see her watching through the slits.

After a few moments of standing there, glowing like anything, the mockingbird dropped into the center of the bushes. Light splashed over the garden, briefly turning the squash and beans into a fantastic landscape of black and white … and then the light was gone.

In the dimness, she could see a figure standing up. The figure bent down, and came up with something in its hand.

Grandma Harken cocked the shotgun. The noise was like a crack of thunder across the desert.

The figure froze.

Grandma Harken looked down the barrel and said, "Don't move. And don't you drop my tomato."

The mockingbird laughed. It was a woman's laugh, short and rueful, but there was a bird's hollowness behind it.

"If you shoot me, it won't be very good for your tomatoes."

"I ain't getting much good out of them at the moment anyway," said Grandma Harken. "Come out from between them, and don't do anything sudden."

"I won't."

She came out from between the plants, still holding the stolen tomato aloft.

Without taking her eyes off her captive, Grandma Harken leaned over and opened the back door. Light flooded out and lit up the face of the mockingbird-woman, where she stood at the foot of the steps.

She was human-shaped, short and broad in the hips, but not human-colored. She had a dark grey back and the white belly of a mockingbird. Her face was grey and black from the lips up, her chin and throat white.

She was naked, but she had feathers instead of hair. Her eyes were starkly orange.

Grandma Harken's hand didn't waver on the shotgun, but her mind was off and running like a jackrabbit.

*She was never born a shapechanger, not looking like that. Whatever she's done or had done to her, it came from the outside in.*

*Huh.*

*Can't imagine why anyone would try to turn herself into a mockingbird, but there's strange people in the world and no accounting for taste.*

*At least she ain't a kachina, or anything that looks like one.* She'd been a trifle worried about that. Grandma Harken's relationship with the people up on the three mesas was distant but cordial and she wanted to keep it that way.

*People get awfully tetchy when you point a shotgun at their spirits.*

Well, you couldn't blame them. If blessed Saint Anthony came walking through the desert, Grandma Harken would've been pretty miffed if somebody shot him full of rock salt.

The shapechanger came up on the porch. She moved slowly, but slowly like a woman who's got a gun pointed at her, not like someone who isn't fitting inside their skin.

"Go on inside," said Grandma Harken. "I'm right behind you."

She got up. The mockingbird-woman glanced at the chair, wired with silverware, and laughed. "So that's how you stayed awake," she said. "Suppose a magic sleep can't compared to a bunch of forks in the back."

*Magic sleep. It wasn't just me getting old. That was a* magic *sleep.*

Grandma did not punch the air and whoop, because that would have been undignified.

Instead she said, "I figured it wasn't natural," and sniffed.

The mockingbird-woman went inside the house. Grandma shut the door and gestured to a chair with the shotgun. "Have a seat."

"You planning on shooting me?" asked her captive.

"Hand over that tomato and I won't shoot anybody."

The mockingbird woman handed over the tomato. Her hands were hard and charcoal-colored, the nails long and diamond shaped. They creased the red skin of the tomato just slightly, but didn't break the surface.

"Why're you stealing them?" she asked.

"Ain't for me," said the mockingbird-woman.

Grandma's eyes flicked to the woman's strange orange ones. "Ah."

"Don't ask me about it," said the woman. "There's not much point." She opened her mouth, and Grandma saw that her tongue was black, and there was a thick silver ring through it.

"Surprised you can talk at all," she said.

The mockingbird-woman shrugged. "You learn to work around it."

Grandma nodded. "So you haven't eaten any of these tomatoes?"

"Not a one. Give you my word."

*And that's another strike against her being born a mockingbird. No member of the crow clan'd hand out their word so lightly.*

She hefted the tomato. She'd made bread earlier in the day, and a little dab of mayonnaise, for the tomato ripening on the counter.

Best to eat it up quick. Neither one would last long in the hot desert air.

"Sit a spell," she said, "and we'll fix that."

Grandma Harken sat at her dinner table with the mockingbird-woman and they ate tomato sandwiches with mayonnaise and a pinch of salt.

It was every bit as good as Grandma Harken had been hoping. The tomato was sweet and acid and firm. It tasted like a morning in summer before the sun burned everything down to the bone.

That tense place in her chest loosened up a little. The world was hard and fierce, but it also contained tomato sandwiches, and if that didn't make it a world worth living in, your standards were unreasonably high.

"So you ain't wearing a mockingbird skin," said Grandma Harken, watching her guest eat up the last crumbs. "You're not taking one off and putting it back on again."

"Nope," said the woman. She licked one of her charcoal fingers and pressed it down on the crumbs, then licked them off again.

"And you were never born that way, either."

"Born same as you," said the woman.

Grandma Harken smiled sourly. "I very much doubt that," she said. "But born human, I guess?"

"You guess right."

"You under some kind of spell, then?"

The mockingbird-woman tapped a fingernail against the silver cuff on her tongue and said nothing.

"Ah," said Grandma. "Well, then. You got a name you can tell me?"

"Marguerite."

"And I'm Grandma Harken. And we're all introduced now. You like being a mockingbird?"

Marguerite stretched. "Don't mind being a bird," she said. "Flying's less fun than you'd think, but it's got its moments. I hate being small, though, and hawks are bastards. And owls." She shuddered, and the feathers on her head all puffed up like a crest. "They don't make a noise when they come up behind you."

Grandma Harken nodded. She respected owls, but she did not want them hanging around the house.

"May I have some water?" asked the mockingbird-woman.

When someone in the desert asks for water, you give it to them. There weren't many rules in the desert, but that was one of them. Grandma Harken got up and poured out a glass for each of them.

Then she made coffee. Between last night and tonight, she was running down to the bottom of her supply, but she had a feeling that Marguerite might appreciate it.

As soon as the smell began to fill the room, she was rewarded. The mockingbird-woman's head lifted and her dark-gray nostrils flared. "Coffee," she said hoarsely.

"I got a little cream to go in it, if you want it."

"Be grateful."

Grandma Harken got out the cream and the sugar, which was nearly as dear as the coffee.

Still, much like tomato sandwiches, there was a time and a place when what you needed was coffee, and nothing else would do.

Grandma poured the coffee out into earthenware mugs and slid the cream across. "From Spangler's cow."

(She did not know why she told the mockingbird-woman this—it seemed unlikely that the odd enchanted creature would be familiar with Spangler or her cow. Still, Grandma felt on some level that if you were drinking something that came out of another living being, you ought to be on a first name basis. The cow in question did not actually have a name, other than "that damn cow," so this was the closest approximation.)

Marguerite wrapped her scaly fingers around the mug and breathed in the steam.

Grandma let her sit in silence with the coffee. When she finally lifted it to her lips, it was a gesture as ritualized and heartfelt as communion.

She closed her eyes and Grandma thought that she might be crying a little, if birds could weep.

*Well. Never underestimate the power of a good cup of coffee.*

She poured herself a cup. Sleep wasn't coming tonight anyway.

"I won't come back," said Marguerite. Her voice was thick. "I'll tell him you caught me. He can get his tomatoes somewhere else—"

Her voice cut off suddenly, with a metallic click, as if the cuff on her tongue had struck her teeth.

"I'd rather they didn't get stolen," said Grandma Harken mildly. It seemed important to talk to fill the sudden silence. "But you're welcome to come back, if you like. I don't mind company."

She considered for a moment, then added, "Well, *specific* company."

Marguerite shook her head. Grandma could see her rolling her tongue around in her mouth, as if trying to find a tender spot. "Not smart," she said, finally.

"Would you be in danger, then?" asked Grandma Harken.

"Nah." She spoke slowly, and Grandma got the impression she was picking each word carefully. "Not really. I'm the only one of me. Can't be another. You understand?"

"Not yet," said Grandma. "But I'm starting to, I think."

She poured out more coffee. Marguerite's hand shook as she added the cream.

"I won't tell anyone you were here, if it matters."

"It won't matter," said the bird-woman. "Too much talking, now." She drank the coffee greedily. "Thank you for this. It's been … a long time."

Grandma Harken nodded.

The light outside the window was starting to edge toward gray. Marguerite looked at it and sighed.

"Should get going," she said.

"You can wait 'til the owls roost, if you want," said Grandma.

"If you don't mind, I'd like that."

*Whatever leash she's on, she's got some slack,* thought Grandma Harken. *But does she want off that leash?*

"Whereabouts you from?" she asked. "Originally, I mean."

"Oh, my." Marguerite leaned back. "North of here a good way. Other side of the Gila."

Grandma Harken nodded. There were towns up that way, although she'd never been out that far. "You got any people up there that might appreciate word?"

Marguerite inhaled sharply.

After a moment, she said, "No. No sense poking old wounds. Thank you for the thought."

"Seems I might have poked one myself. I'm sorry."

Marguerite set down the coffee cup. "No harm done."

She rose. Grandma Harken saw her only chance slipping away, and decided to be blunt. "You're got one leg in a trap," she said. "You want it opened?"

"No one can open it," said Marguerite.

"If somebody could, though?"

"It's too dangerous—"

"I'm a lot older than you, and a lot meaner," said Grandma Harken, annoyed. "And I don't take kindly to being lectured by a tomato thief. I ain't promising you anything and you ain't asking me for anything. Just yes or no."

The mockingbird-woman stared at her for a moment, then her lips widened in an unwilling grin. Her teeth were shockingly white against her black bird's tongue.

"I'd give it all," she said. "But now I've got to go."

"Go slow," said Grandma Harken. "And watch for owls."

She opened the door. Marguerite went down the steps and her skin blazed suddenly silver. By the time she reached the bottom step, she was shrinking, as if she were hunching down.

Then she was a mockingbird again. She took three hops on the dusty garden path and launched herself into the air.

Grandma Harken nodded to her and raised a hand. The fiery bird flew to the top of the garden gate, and then away.

"Well," said Grandma Harken. "Good thing I put on my good boots." She snatched up the bag by the door, opened the bedroom so that Spookcat could get to water, and took her walking stick into her hand.

Then she opened the garden gate and followed the spark of fire into the desert.

By the time the sun came up, Grandma Harken was hot and thirsty and tired.

Her water bottle was nearly empty. She had lost the mockingbird twice, and then found her again as she took flight. But now it seemed that she had lost her for good.

She was well up in the desert now, and there was something strange going on in the air.

It wasn't anything you'd notice if you weren't looking for it. A little bit of heat haze in a place that couldn't be hot enough yet to ripple. A wash that had water in it, except that Grandma knew damn well that it didn't, not this time of year. Palo verde needles that moved in a wind that wasn't happening anywhere near here.

You had to know the desert well, or have a good sense of the uncanny. Grandma had both and she didn't like it.

"Blessed Saint Anthony," she muttered. "Somebody's folding the world."

There wasn't any rhyme or reason to it, as near as she could tell. It didn't look deliberate. It seemed to follow in the wake of the mockingbird.

*Two places lying close together, and sometimes you put your foot through one and into the other. Whatever she's doing, she's moving in between 'em.*

There wasn't anything terrible in that other place, so far as Grandma knew—or at least, nothing that wasn't already terrible in this one. It wasn't anymore full of monsters than anywhere else. It was just a little bit different. The places bled into each other all the time. It wasn't at all unnatural.

It was damned inconvenient, though, if you were trying to track a thing the size of a mockingbird.

She stomped over the sand, leaving tracks that were mostly bootprints. Sometimes the world folded around them and the tracks were bare feet.

Once or twice they belonged to a jackrabbit.

She stopped at last, taking another drink of water, and looked around. It was going to be a long way back. If the one wash was still full when she passed it again, she'd have to drink a little water from it.

*And it'll give me the runs, too, like as not.*

The bird was nowhere to be seen. The hillside was an intricate pattern of white powdered earth between dark green scrub.

The first cicada began to buzz, and its brethren chimed in, until the air was a long rattling hiss of heat.

There were two long metal rails across the ground on the opposite hillside. A little green scribble of a weed had grown up along the slope, but nothing grew between the tracks.

When she breathed in, she could smell it faintly—the hot gunmetal smell of the train-god.

The tracks ran off toward the horizon. The burning mockingbird was nowhere to be seen.

Grandma exhaled. "Well," she said. She spoke out loud, so the tracks could hear her, just in case something was listening. "Well. Guess it's time to go pay a call on the Mother of Trains."

She walked back into town, which took long enough to convince her that she didn't want to walk clear to the train station. She swung by her house, fed Spook-cat, and left a note for Eva. Then she set out for the stable.

It was a good stable, kept clean, and it was run by a man named Tomas, who had gotten tomato seeds from Grandma Harken on three separate occasions. This was a rare benediction, and he was careful not to take it for granted.

"I need your old mule," Grandma Harken told him. "The one I like to ride."

Tomas looked at her, gazed briefly heavenward, and said, "That mule died five years ago, Abuela Harken."

Grandma blinked. "What'd he die of?"

"Old age," said Tomas, who was always extremely respectful but had a sense of humor anyway.

"Huh!"

After a minute she said, "What's the next oldest mule you got?"

"I've got a *young* mule," said Tomas, "who's as polite a girl as you'll ever meet. And you are welcome to ride her, Abuela."

"I like the old ones," said Grandma, disgruntled.

"She'll get old in due time."

Grandma glared at him. Tomas contrived to look innocent.

"Fine," said Grandma. "But she better have good manners."

"She has better manners than my sons, Abuela."

Grandma muttered to herself. Tomas had two sons, who were polite and respectful and built like bulls and who would spend hours splitting firewood for an old lady. These were things you learned to appreciate when you were Grandma Harken's age.

The mule was indeed very well-mannered. She pricked her ears up and lipped delicately at Grandma's sleeve.

"Good girl," said Grandma, petting her nose. "Is she smart?" she asked Tomas.

"She's a mule."

"I've known some stupid mules."

"A stupid mule is still smarter than a good horse or a bad man."

Grandma sighed. It can be annoying when other people are right.

She loaded water bottles onto the mule and climbed on.

The mule waited politely—*Is this everything? That's all?*—then set out. Grandma clicked her tongue and flipped the reins, setting her on the road to the next town over.

The one that had a train station.

The desert was full of strange things, but the trains were some of the strangest.

When white men came to lay iron rails across the land, the land didn't take kindly to it. The train tracks looked too much like chains. The land brought heat and death and disease, and work on the rails slowed to a crawl.

"So they brought us to die instead," said Grandma's friend Anna. "From Canton to San Francisco and out to here." She swept her hands when she said it, taking in the province across the ocean that she had never seen, and the desert where she had lived all her life.

That was the truth of history. Hundreds came and thousands died and hundreds more came to replace them. The blood of Anna's people had bathed every inch of the rails.

When the train-gods woke, it was no wonder who they chose to be their priests. Chinese, black, Irish—even a Cornish woman way up north, where the snow piled up everywhere but on the tracks. People who had, with toil and tears, earned the gods' regard.

It had made a lot of big money men back east furious. They thought they'd owned the railroads. They had the pull to get the army brought out to try and bring the machines back under their control.

The train-gods only had to eat a couple of regiments before they realized their mistake.

*Lotta damn foolishness,* Grandma Harken thought. *People ought to be a lot quicker to listen to each other and a little slower to listen to something that calls itself a god.*

She wouldn't have said that out loud, though. She didn't want it getting back to a train, or worse yet, to Anna.

Anyway, the system worked. You could get a train from one side of the country to the other, though it wasn't always the same train or even the same country out the windows. Freight got moved, more or less. Sometimes it wound up in the wrong place or was summarily dumped in the middle of nowhere. The machines were capricious gods. (This was part of the reason for the price of coffee.)

They were very good about letters, though. Anna's grandson was the current train-priest, and he said that his god thought letters were prayers and moved them as a kind of professional courtesy.

You appreciated that sort of thing in a god.

Grandma Harken could afford to be a little detached. Her people hadn't been involved one way or the other. It had all been long, long before her time.

It'd been a good bit before Anna's time too, truth be told, but Anna had an image to maintain.

Neither Anna nor any of her grandchildren could have said what bargain the train-gods struck with the desert, though.

That there was a bargain was undeniable. Grandma Harken herself had noticed that the tracks took some odd turns sometimes, to avoid a wash or a particular stone—turns that no human would have introduced to the line. And it was true that you could walk the rails until you died of thirst, and you'd never see the shadow of a saguaro lying over the tracks.

What it all meant, though, Grandma left for others to decide. The bargain was between the desert and the trains, and no business of any mortal creature at all.

Anna looked old. She was younger than Grandma Harken—probably—but neither of them were quick to compare.

She lived in a house alongside the train station. It was an old adobe, same as all the other houses in town, but it had a brightly painted balcony on the second floor and faded lanterns hung from the ends of the corner beams.

One of her grandchildren—or great-grandchildren, Grandma wasn't sure, and after the bit with the mule, she'd rather not find out—opened the carved wooden door and let Grandma Harken inside. Anna was sitting in a chair in one corner of the room, her feet up on a stool.

"Harken?" she said. "Is that you, you old jackrabbit?"

"Last I looked," said Grandma Harken. "You still alive?"

"Looks that way. Come in." She waved to the grandchild and a chair was produced. "What brings you here?"

"Need an answer, and maybe a favor."

Anna raised an eyebrow. She had very little left in the way of eyebrows, but her face was so wrinkled that the gesture remained effective. "If you've come to ask for a train to fetch your grandson home, I'd advise against it."

"Lord, no!"

Anna relaxed. "Glad to hear it. I'm still surprised we didn't have some broody little babies around here nine months later."

"He didn't brood as a baby." Grandma paused, remembering. "Well. Much."

Anna laughed.

"Sit, sit. Have you eaten? Are you thirsty?"

The answers to these questions were completely immaterial—food and tea would be forthcoming anyway. Grandma Harken let herself sink into the comfort of Anna's hospitality.

She'd brought along a half-dozen nearly ripe tomatoes. Now that she'd finally eaten one, they weren't so precious to her.

The tomatoes were duly admired and whisked away into the kitchen. Tea was drunk, then more tea, and then Grandma Harken held up her hands and said, "No more, Anna, I'm begging you. I'll explode."

Anna laughed. "All right. You came for an answer, then."

Grandma nodded.

"A woman," she said. "Turned into a mockingbird, from up past Gila way."

Anna tilted her head. "Not one of mine."

"Wouldn't think so. But some kind of enchanter's got her bound up with a silver cuff through her tongue, and I aim to break her loose if I can. She called it a 'he' but that's all I know."

She sat back, and glanced at the windows out of habit.

"Nothing out there can hear you," said Anna. "Or if it could, it's so big that you shouldn't be tangling with it anyhow." She flicked her fingers. "Sounds interesting, but what do you need with the Mother of Trains?"

Grandma told her about the tracks.

"I could go over every inch of the desert and miss it if somebody folded the world up the wrong way," she said. "Trains don't care about folds."

"They run in three worlds," said Anna distantly. "We will not talk about the fourth. If there is anything to be seen, the train-gods will see it."

She gestured, and the grandchild appeared. Grandma Harken took the time to finally look at the child—a girl, delicate as a quail, probably older than she looked. "Go and get your uncle," Anna said. "Tell him we will be at the station shortly, with a question."

The girl nodded and padded away.

Anna watched her go. Someone would have to have known her as long as Grandma Harken to notice the sudden smoothing of a line between her eyes, as if she had found an answer that eluded her.

"The next priest?" asked Grandma.

"I wouldn't wish it on her," said Anna wearily. "She's got desert in her, not steel."

Grandma nodded. She was something of an authority on the subject.

"I'll send her to you," said Anna.

"Like hell you will!" Grandma scowled over her tea. "I don't need a girl and I'm hard to live with. And I'll probably die running after mockingbirds."

"Then you'll want somebody to point to where the body fell," said Anna. She waved a hand. "Not now. Later. Soon, I think, but not yet. After you've dealt with this foolishness, perhaps."

"I said—"

"You get your answer and she gets a teacher," said Anna. "Fair trade."

Grandma Harken glowered, but she knew that Anna had her in a hard place. And the girl like a quail needed ... something.

"She broke her arm when she was small," said Anna quietly. "She's got cholla ribs for bones. We didn't let the doctor see. I set it myself."

Grandma sucked the air in between her teeth. That was immense power and vulnerability, all at once. That was a child that should never be taken out of the desert.

That was someone a little more like Grandma Harken than either of them were like fully human folk.

"Dammit, Anna ..."

"Dammit, yourself."

Anna's grandson Jun was a slender man with apologetic eyes. He clasped his hands together and bowed over them to Grandma Harken. "How may I assist you, Grandmother?"

It felt awkward to be formal with a man you'd seen in diapers, but Grandma Harken had come to speak to a train-priest, not talk about how much he'd grown in the last forty years. She nodded to him. "Appreciate it, Jun. Looking to see if the train's gone past anything strange."

They stood in the station itself, not the main platform, but the small room before it where the train priest spoke to the engines.

There was no train there now, which was a relief. A train was like having a thunderstorm in the room with you, and having a priest around made it worse.

Jun smiled ruefully. "The trains go past many strange things, Grandmother."

"One in particular, then," said Grandma, and set out to describe the place where the world was folded and the train tracks ran through it.

Jun listened. He listened intently, with his eyes closed, and Grandma had to fight to keep from shivering.

*Passing right through him to something else. It ain't natural.*

And then, because she had to be fair: *Lot of good things ain't natural. Most of 'em just don't rub your face in it.*

She finished describing it and waited.

"Yesssss . . ." said Jun, and there was a hiss of brake lines in it. "Yessss, I ssee."

He opened his eyes. Grandma'd seen it once before, so she didn't take a step back, even if a good chunk of her skin wanted to.

It was nothing so dramatic as the color changing. It was only that there was something else in his eyes, something that wasn't human or even close to it. When he blinked, his eyelids came down like the door to the firebox slamming shut.

"Along the line," he said. "North and west and north again. There are five saguaros together. There is a hill of stones. There is a dwelling of the used-up people. There is a person there." He nodded twice, with his eyes still closed. "There is nothing else for many miles."

"This person," said Grandma Harken, "he's folding the world?"

Sweat was beginning to trickle down Jun's face. She could feel the heat radiating off him. "There is a person. There is a bend in the track. There is a bend in the track."

"Does that mean—"

*"There is a bend in the track."*

Anna put a hand on Grandma's arm and shook her head.

Grandma bowed to her friend's experience. "Thank you," she said.

The train-god, through Jun, said "Yesssss …" and it trailed away into the distance as the god went away again.

Jun stood for a moment, trembling like a horse that has run a hard race, then let out his breath in a long sigh. When he opened his eyes, they were only human dark.

"Can you tell me what it meant by *there is a bend in the track?"* asked Grandma.

Jun took out a cloth and wiped his head. "It's hard to say," he said. "Probably there's really a bend, but repeating it like that …" He shook his head. "They fixate on odd things. That was the *Mariposa*. It's not the clearest of the trains. *Leviathan* was better, but *Leviathan* has stopped speaking. The other trains say that it's waiting for something."

This was alarming, but also nothing to do with Grandma Harken. She made a mental note to order more coffee, though, in case the trains were planning to run mad.

They left the station. Jun came with them, not sweating now, shivering as if it were midnight in the desert instead of noon. Anna sent another grandchild to get him tea and put a blanket around his shoulders herself.

"Worth it?" she asked Grandma.

"I hope so," said Grandma. "Thank you, Jun."

The girl with bones made of cholla ribs said, "Who are the used-up people?"

"Hohokam," said Grandma, which was a thing she hadn't known she knew until she said it. "The ones who built all the canals. That's what their name means, the used-up ones. Our enchanter's squatting in some ruins, I guess."

"Do you think he's Hohokam, then?" asked Anna.

"Not unless he's a thousand years old," said Grandma. "Which I can't rule out entirely. I'll be going. Jun, thank you, and you too,

Anna." Her eyes slid over the cholla-bone girl and she nodded once and took her leave.

She rode back to Tomas's stable with her mind full of shards, like a shattered clay pot. The Hohokam were all jumbled up with the trains and the folded world and the girl and the mockingbird.

Well, no matter. Things would sort themselves out. She'd know what she had to know when she needed it.

"Or I'll get caught with my pants around my ankles," she said to the mule's ears, "and I'll die with a stupid expression on my face. I suppose that counts as getting sorted out, though."

The mule flicked her ears, but did not comment.

"I suppose I better try not to die," she said after a little while. "That girl of Anna's is gonna need some teaching."

She tried to think about what she could teach anyone, let alone a girl who was already part of the desert, and the thought was overwhelming. She hadn't been all that good with her own baby, and Eva had been as good and placid and easy a child as any born.

It was late when she reached the stable. A light burned in the window, though, and after a moment the door slammed, and one of Tomas's sons came out to meet her.

"You didn't have to stay up," she said. "I might've been gone days."

"We would have stayed up for you, Abuela Harken," said Tomas's son. He looped the mule's reins over his hand and led her into her stall.

There was nothing much to say to kindness, particularly when you suspect that it's because you're old. Grandma walked the rest of the way, to the house with its back like the desert.

"At least I'll get one more night in my own bed," she said. "With my own Spook-cat on the pillow. Can't ask for more than that."

In the end she got two more nights. The garden was wreathed in beans and the little green husks of tomatillos were beginning to dangle from the sprawling plants. They needed staking. If Grandma Harken had known beyond a shadow of a doubt that she was going to die tomorrow, she would still have staked up the tomatillos and harvested the beans.

She had two ripe tomatoes and she ate them both, on bread with salt, and they were perfect.

On the morning of the second day, she got up before dawn. She petted Spook-cat, which first alarmed, and then delighted him. She strapped water bottles to herself like a bandolier and filled her pockets with sage and cigarettes; she put on her good boots and wrote a note for her daughter that said "I love you," and then she closed the garden gate behind her and walked into the desert.

The pre-dawn air was sharp and gray and seamless. There were no mockingbirds to light her way. Still, here, she didn't need them. This was a landscape she knew as well as she knew her own name.

The folds in the world that had gone out from the mockingbird's wings had settled now, a paper ball crumpled and then smoothed out again. There were still small ridges here and there. Grandma Harken could see them if she looked—the shadow of a palo verde tree that fell a handspan too short, a place where, for an instant, there were two moons in the sky. But these were small things.

She reached the train tracks as the sun came up. It dyed the rails rose and chrome. Grandma Harken stood, thoughtful, and took a long drink of water.

"All right," she muttered to herself. "All right. If I were a train . . ."

It was dangerous to walk on train tracks now. A train could appear out of nowhere, skipping from one world to the next, and give you only a bare moment of warning.

Still, it was no more dangerous than anything else. She cleared her throat and spoke to the rails: "The Mother of Trains knows my name."

There was no overt acknowledgement. She hadn't expected one. She stepped up onto the rails and began to walk between them. Her boots made a satisfying clomping sound on the railroad ties.

The desert heated rapidly. She passed saguaro standing tall, arms raised, filled with woodpecker holes. A thrasher called from the top of one, and she had to shade her eyes and see if it was actually a mockingbird.

There were no shadows on the tracks. The saguaros folded their arms to prevent it, and they were the only thing tall enough to cast a shadow here.

She walked until the sky was turquoise hard, until she had emptied one water bottle and begun another. Then she shaded her eyes and looked ahead, and there were five saguaros standing together, and a hill beyond them, crusted with stones.

Grandma Harken nodded to herself.

The tracks did bend there, an abrupt turn that no train that was not a god could have navigated. The metal rails held together, but the wooden ties were twisted up as if they were made of dough and not creosote-soaked wood.

*There is a bend in the tracks.*

"Quite a bend, too," she said aloud.

A coyote trotted by, ears alert. It glanced at her, interested, and flicked its brush.

"Don't you start," she added.

The coyote grinned, that being the natural expression of coyotes. It trotted on.

She walked back and forth along the bend, and absolutely nothing happened.

"Huh," she said. She'd been hoping … well, nothing was ever easy.

She went back a third time.

The coyote was back. Its eyes were the coldest thing in the desert.

She couldn't see any edges. The shadows on the hill were clean and crisp.

The coyote was circling her.

*I'm not looking to die just yet. Go find some other meat.*

She knew that coyotes couldn't hear thoughts, but sometimes she thought they could smell them. It winked at her, and then it passed on the far side of the tracks and vanished completely.

Grandma Harken grunted.

"I'll be damned," she said aloud.

Well. The enchanter—whatever or whoever he was—had folded up the world here, folded it so hard that it doubled back on itself, so that something on the far side vanished completely from view. The tracks had pulled away from the fold, like skin sloughing away from a burn.

*The trains run in three worlds. We will not speak of the fourth.*

*Dammit, Anna.*

Suppose the enchanter had folded all three worlds around him, to keep the trains away, and was living in the fourth world?

"Blessed Saint Anthony ..."

The coyote reappeared on the far side of the hill. It trotted up to the tracks and sat down, tongue lolling, God's dog amused at something.

*Waiting to see how I do, I suppose.*

She studied the hill carefully. It looked like any other small hillside in a desert, not large enough to be a mesa, merely a rise in the landscape, dotted with mesquite and teddy-bear cholla. An ocotillo spread a hundred fantastical arms near the base, where there might be a small seep of some sort. Ocotillo liked more water than other plants, when they could get it.

If there was water here, the Hohokam might have built near it. If there were a people better at using water in the desert, Grandma had never heard of it.

The hill had nothing that looked like ruins, though, not even two square stones beside each other. Not a temple mound nor—

Her eyes narrowed. The coyote tilted its head.

On a rock above the ocotillo, there was a pale splotch. She ambled over to it, and there it was, pecked out of the surface, a round-bodied lizard.

"So they were here," she murmured. Her eyes tracked over the petroglyphs—a human, a set of concentric circles, another lizard, bigger than the last one. A human upside down, which generally meant "dead."

The coyote had stopped grinning and was watching her intently.

"Don't suppose you can tell me anything," said Grandma Harken.

"What'll you give me?" replied the coyote.

"I've got sage and cigarettes."

The coyote scratched pensively at one ear. "Let's see the cigarettes."

Grandma Harken took one out and laid it on a stone, then stepped back.

The coyote sniffed at it, unimpressed. "Poor stuff."

"You eat sheep afterbirths," said Grandma.

"Yes, but only the quality ones," said the coyote, and grinned again.

"I should know better than to try and deal with coyotes," muttered Grandma Harken.

"You should." The coyote licked up the cigarette and held it dangling in its mouth. "Look! I'm a human. Do this. Do that. Stand here. Don't eat that." It cackled at its own cleverness.

Grandma Harken shook her head and turned back to the railroad tracks.

"Go underneath," called the coyote after her, and when she turned her head back toward it, it was gone.

*Go underneath.* She turned the words over in her mind. *Go underneath.*

Coyotes were liars, of course. Worse than ravens. But this one had taken the tobacco.

She walked along the track, into the sharp bend. The rails buckled, and the gaps between the ties were deeper than they should have been. And yet the hillside was seamless, not even a shadow out of place.

*Almost perfect,* she thought. *No one would ever notice, if not for the trains.*

She stood at the farthest point of the bend, a foot on each tie. The world dropped away underneath the rails.

*Go underneath.*

The gap should have been too narrow for a grown human to fit, but one of the ties was twisted out of the way, on the end nearest the ruins. And she was made of bone and sinew and wire, and was no longer young.

She wiped sweat from her palms, grabbed the metal rail—it was hot from the sun and burned her hands—and swung herself down through the gap, and into the next world.

Immediately everything changed.

The hillside was no longer a small rise but a large one, cleft in two, with a narrow stone defile between them. Petroglyphs marked the stones on either side, layered over each other into incoherence.

Grandma Harken took out her water bottle and spilled a little over her smarting palms.

She turned her head and the tracks were gone. That was going to make getting out … interesting.

"Oh well," she muttered. "If I were sensible, I'd still be at home with my tomatoes." She started forward into the defile.

There was a dragon in the sand.

It was thirty yards long, thick bodied, with a blunt wedge of head. Its scales were dusty black and mottled orange.

Grandma knew Gila monsters well enough and did not fear them, but the largest one that she had ever seen was smaller than the smallest claw on this one's foot.

"Oh," she said aloud. "Oh, my."

She heard herself say it and hated her voice for sounding like an old woman. But even Saint Anthony, who wrestled demons in the desert, might have been taken aback by the size of this one.

The dragon's eyes were glossy, beetle shell black, and they were fixed on her.

She swallowed hard.

"Give me water," said the Gila dragon, in a voice like sand hissing over the desert floor.

"Jesus, Mary, and Joseph," said Grandma Harken, but she sounded more like herself in her ears.

"They are not here," said the dragon, "or I would ask them for water."

And it laughed, then, a little choking hiss, and it seemed to Grandma that it was the sound of a creature in pain, not a monster on the edge of devouring a victim.

*Not that that won't change in very short order, mind you …*

Grandma Harken unfastened one of her water bottles. She suspected that she was going to die very shortly, but there were rules. If she lived long enough to talk to the cholla-bone girl again, she would tell her this one.

*When someone in the desert asks you for water, you give it to them.*

The Gila dragon's mouth cracked open and a long blue-violet tongue slithered out towards Grandma.

She upended the water bottle over it.

The dragon swallowed, and then there was a crack like thunder.

She hadn't noticed the shackles on the dragon's leg. They were the same dusty black color as the scales.

There were three of them. Two still held, and the third had broken and fallen away. The skin underneath was raw and clear fluid oozed from beneath the scales.

"Give me water," whispered the dragon.

She gave it the next water bottle to drink.

The second shackle broke. She could not see where the chain was anchored. To hold a beast that size, they must have been bolted to the center of the earth itself.

"Give me water," said the dragon a third time.

*One shackle left. And when it breaks, it could lunge forward and devour me. It wouldn't even need the poison. One bite ought to do it.*

Only a fool would set such a monster free.

"Please," said the Gila dragon.

Grandma Harken cursed herself for a fool and poured the last of her water out over the dragon's tongue.

The crack that followed was louder than the others and split the air like lightning, like the sound of mountains splitting.

In the silence that followed, she heard the tiny metallic *clunk* of the shackle falling to the ground.

The dragon looked down at its freed leg. That would have been the moment to run, but Grandma Harken thought perhaps she should just sit down. Her heart was hammering in a way that she didn't like, and her vision pulsed in time to her heartbeat.

*It'd be entirely too stupid, to drop dead of a heart attack out here in the desert before the beast lays a claw on me.*

It lifted its great mottled head. It was a low, flat beast, for all its size, so it did not tower over her. She looked into its eye and saw her face reflected back.

"Thank you," said the dragon. And waited, like a penitent awaiting absolution.

Grandma licked her lips. "Weren't nothing," she said.

It moved then. She fell back against the canyon wall and watched it go by. It was like a train-god passing, long and dark, and then it was past and the bright blunt tail was vanishing around the curve of the defile. She heard the sound of its scales scraping the stone, and then, much too quickly for something so large, it was gone.

*Stepped out the world,* she thought, *back into one of the other ones. I hope it doesn't get hung up on the rails.*

She slid down until she was sitting and put her forehead on her knees. There had been a time, when she was young and immortal, when beasts like that were part of her world and she could have danced in the tracks that they left in the sand.

She felt old and mortal now.

She had a few sips of water left in one of the bottles. When the pulsing sparks in her eyes faded, she drank one of the last sips.

She got up.

There was a scale on the ground before her. Not a large one, a little smaller than her palm. She picked it up, and it was warm and felt like leather. She put it in her pocket, because sometimes the desert gives you an answer, and it is your job to find the question.

She had to keep one hand on the stone wall as she walked. She could feel chisel marks under her fingers. The way was mostly natural, but someone had smoothed down the stone a little, long ago.

Grandma Harken followed the turn in the wall and there it was.

It was adobe and it was old. The roof had fallen in on one side and the tops of the walls had the slumped-pottery look of weathered clay.

It was not a large building. The entire structure was not much larger than Grandma's house, though it had been at least three stories tall before the roof fell. If she tilted her head back, she could see the remains of shattered floors sticking out from the high, broken wall.

The world was folded so tightly around it that the desert sun had turned the hazy gray-green color of the sky before a storm.

There was trash around the outside. Bird bones and rotting scraps of fruit made a scattered midden, although she could not smell anything. A few flat weeds crawled across the ground and despite everything, Grandma Harken felt a gardener's urge to pull them.

*Not the time. Although if I don't die in the next few hours, I'll get them before I leave.*

The opening to the ruins was a narrow rectangle of darkness. She watched it for a long time before she approached it.

She had taken only a step or two forward when someone came out.

He was young, perhaps in his late teens, and clad in the same strange, feathered skin that Marguerite had been. By that, she thought he was likely a victim. He had a dark crest and his cheeks were stained brilliant scarlet.

*Roadrunner*, thought Grandma Harken.

He saw her.

His mouth fell open in surprise—she saw a glint of silver in his tongue—and he said something frantic in O'odham.

Grandma could understand about twenty words of O'odham if the other person spoke very slowly and clearly, which he hadn't.

*Probably warning me off. He's not the enchanter, anyhow. Poor kid must have gotten caught like Marguerite.*

*He does like turning people into birds, doesn't he?*

From inside the ruin came another voice, thick and rumbling. She could not tell what it said, either, but the roadrunner-boy put his hands to his mouth and grimaced.

"It's all right," she said. She'd never had much of a plan anyway, and apparently stealth wasn't part of it.

Whether he understood her words or her tone, she didn't know. He took her arm, his eyes apologetic. She followed him inside.

It took a long moment for her eyes to adjust. The gray-green light through the broken ceiling did little to illuminate the shadows.

It was colder inside the ruin than it should have been.

"Ah, hell," said Marguerite, somewhere off to her left. "I told you to stay away."

"I'm bad at that," said Grandma cheerfully, as she tried to pierce the darkness.

There were broken pots in the corners, and a few intact ones, draped with old flower sacks and coarse-cured hides. It smelled rank. Whoever lived here was a poor housekeeper.

At the far end, something moved.

She heard the thick, rumbling voice again. This time, it spoke English.

"Where do you come from, old woman?" asked the voice. "And why are you sniffing around what is mine?"

Her first thought was that it was a bear.

Her second was that bears generally had better manners, and certainly kept themselves cleaner.

It was a man, more or less. He was huge and hairy and his head was sunk down between his shoulders. He sat on a throne, like a king, but the throne was made of broken stones and rabbit skins and there were flies crawling in and out of it.

He did not belong in the desert. He stank of cold and forests and distance, of magic from another place and another time. More than that, he stank of power—his own power, wrapped up in that bear-like hide, not a power that could give itself to a place and be given back in return.

There were things that could come to the desert and learn to live with it, like the trains, but this was not one of them.

"You're not from around here," said Grandma Harken to the cold-king.

He made a noise like bubbles breaking in glue, and maybe that was laughter.

"I have been driven out," he said. "Someone found the soul I had hidden in a duck egg. It takes time to grow it back."

"Seems a fragile sort of place for a soul," said Grandma Harken. "Better than a chicken egg, but not by much."

"I shall wrap it in a snake next time," said the cold-king. "I have learned."

Marguerite and the roadrunner boy shifted in the corner. Grandma spared them a look and saw that Marguerite had put her arms around the boy for comfort.

*Well, and now I know why she wasn't entirely keen on curse-breaking. Had nothing much to do with flying after all.*

She had no idea what she was going to do, but it seemed like she should probably start doing it.

"I'll ask politely," said Grandma Harken. "Let these people go and stop twisting up the world hereabouts. The land doesn't like it." She considered this, and then added, "Please."

"I do not care what the land likes," said the cold-king. "This is a dreadful land."

"Then why'd you come here at all?"

The cold-king stretched. "I did not choose. I hid myself in the seeds of a thistle and when I woke again, I had crossed an ocean and was rolling and rolling across the hills of this terrible, dry place. But soon I shall be done growing back, and until then, my old enemies will not find me."

Grandma Harken sighed. She had never thought it was going to be easy. "Well," she said, planting her feet, "I'm afraid you've made a new one."

The cold-king flung out his arm and power raged through the ruined building. Marguerite cried out and the roadrunner-boy spoke a short, sharp curse.

The cold-king's power struck Grandma Harken and would have knocked her down, but she let it spin her around instead. She'd been a dancer in her youth, the wild kind, so she spun like a top and landed, breathless, on her feet.

*Well, this is going to end badly,* she thought.

Her right hip let it be known that it was not up for any more of that.

She reached down and pulled out her kitchen knife. It had seemed very large when cutting tomatoes in her kitchen. Now it was a small bright wedge against the bulk of the cold-king.

He laughed his bubbling laugh again. "Pretty," he said.

The next blow came sideways and there was no spinning with it. It slammed her into the ruined adobe wall. Her head struck it and spawned a universe of stars across her vision. The knife went skittering across the floor.

She slid down the wall and into a jumble of shattered pots. One dug into her back, in the same place that the ladle had, and for a moment Grandma wondered if she was still in her chair on the porch, watching a glowing bird fly across the garden.

*Was that a dream? The dragon and the train and …*

She remembered the cholla-bone girl's face. No, she had not been a dream. Her mouth was full of blood.

"No!" cried Marguerite. The mockingbird-woman lunged across the floor, her orange eyes shining in the dark. She caught the cold-king's arm and tugged at it, fierce and ineffectual. "Stop! She's old! She can't hurt you!"

*Shows what you know*, thought Grandma, vague and indignant. She didn't think she could stand up, but she wasn't done yet. She'd hurt that bastard plenty.

She would … she would …

She had no idea what she was going to do.

She had lost her knife. She put her hand in her pocket, looking for something else—a weapon, a seed, she didn't know what—and found something smooth and leathery under her fingers.

The cold-king flicked Marguerite off as if she were a fly. She landed on her shoulder, and the roadrunner-boy ran to her and crouched over her, fierce and futile.

Grandma Harken pulled the leathery thing out of her pocket. It was the scale from the dragon.

The cold-king turned his head, snorting. "What is that?" he said, sounding surprised, and it occurred to Grandma for the first time that he might not know that she had freed the monster.

He lifted his hand. She could not flee, and she could not dodge, and she was already against the wall. The next blow would likely kill her, for her bones were no longer as strong as they had been.

For lack of anything better to do, she put the scale in her mouth and bit down hard. The musty reptile taste mixed with the salt of blood, a thin, acrid stew.

There was another crack of thunder, like the sound of the shackles breaking, and something struck the wall of the old adobe.

The cold-king turned, startled. Pebbles rattled from the ceiling.

It occurred to Grandma Harken that she should probably get up before the ceiling came down.

She rolled sideways, slowly, onto her knees. She did not seem to be dead yet.

The wall shuddered under another impact. There were cracks in the wall now, running in all directions.

She stood up. Her back felt like an open wound.

The wall fell.

Through the gap came sunlight, thin and hazy as it was in this place. She saw the blunt wedge of the Gila dragon's head, and then it drew back and slammed forward like a hammer.

The cold-king blinked in the sudden light. His face was fish-belly white under the coat of hair.

She looked around for something to throw at him—it didn't have to be large, just a distraction, anything to buy the dragon another few moments—and then the roadrunner-boy charged.

The sound he made was half-human, half-bird.

The cold-king slapped at the air, and another wave of power washed over them, but differently.

The roadrunner-boy fell down and was a roadrunner. Marguerite's cry became the harsh scold of a mockingbird. And Grandma Harken, who had been hunched over, searching for a weapon, dropped back to all fours, her body twisting into a shape at once forgotten and familiar.

Her ribs heaved. Her ears were as long as her arms. Two sickle horns rose up on her brow. Her fur was white with age, but her legs quivered with the memory of speed.

*Well.* Well. *It's been a long time.*

She would have laughed then, but jackrabbits don't.

The cold-king stared at her. "You were supposed to be a bird," he said, sounding baffled. For a moment he sounded less like a monster and more like a man. "They're *always* birds."

The dragon hit the wall again and it fell down and took part of the roof with it.

Grandma stamped. She couldn't help it. She had no other way to shout a warning. The roadrunner ran for the open doorway, and the mockingbird fluttered, dodging falling stone.

The cold-king spun around as masonry struck him, and the Gila dragon reached in and closed its jaws over him.

Grandma winced.

The poison of a Gila monster is greatly exaggerated. The bite is not. It clamped down on the cold-king and no power on earth could have freed him.

The cold-king sagged like a puppet with its strings cut. There was no blood at all.

Grandma stamped again, because the deathless do not die so easily. From the doorway, the roadrunner and the mockingbird looked in.

The body heaved. Around the edge of the dragon's teeth, the flesh gaped open and something fell out.

It was a hare, but it looked unfinished. It was hairless, though its eyes were open. It staggered as it tried to walk, and its legs wobbled.

*Until I finish growing back*, the cold-king had said.

*Not quite finished, then,* thought Grandma, and launched herself at the hare.

She was old but her claws were still sharp. She struck the hare hard and rolled it over, biting at its throat.

Its flesh was soft and spongy, slick with fluid. She could not get purchase on it. It did not fight back but squirmed against her, trying to escape, leave a trail of slime like a slug over her paws.

It wiggled a little way free and the mockingbird struck at its eyes. Grandma ignored the screaming of old bones and grappled with it again, kicking for its belly.

Her claws found purchase at last, and tore into the swollen skin. Again, there was no blood. The hare's body went limp and something feathered fought its way free from the open belly.

She did not know what kind of bird it was—some sort of water fowl, with a harlequin mask of green and cream over its face. She struck at it, tearing strips from its wing, but it was in the air before she could bring it down.

It made it nearly to the open doorway and the mockingbird slammed into its head.

Marguerite, in bird form, was barely a third the size of the fowl, but she fought like a creature possessed, battering the creature's face with its wings, keeping it out of the air. The fowl hissed like a snake, trying to get into the canyon and more open air.

Grandma dragged herself forward. If she leapt, she could knock it out of the air—if she could even leap. It did not seem likely. Kicking the hare open had done things to her hips that would be a long time healing.

The roadrunner slammed into the fowl's back, driving its long beak into the fowl's neck. It went limp.

*And is that all?*

*No. It never is, is it?*

Its bill opened and the neck worked as if the corpse were vomiting. A serpent with tiny, poisonous eyes slithered free, tail whipping as it fled.

The roadrunner pounced before it had gotten three feet away. Of all the prey in the desert, it was snakes that they loved the most.

It seized the beast behind the head and whipped it back and forth against the canyon wall.

Grandma sat back on her haunches, tense and trembling, waiting for the next form.

The snake's body split open and a white egg flew out.

It traced a pale arc in the air, glistening. The roadrunner dropped the snake. The mockingbird flung herself into the air after it. The ancient horned jackrabbit lunged forward.

And the coyote with cold-moon eyes caught it neatly out of the air and swallowed it in two bites.

"What?" it said, licking its lips. "Were you going to eat that?"

The air shivered. The folds fell away as three worlds snapped back into place. The sky was blue and hard instead of hazy green. Grandma was an old woman sitting on the side of a hill, with her legs tucked up beneath her. Marguerite fell heavily out of the air and the roadrunner boy helped her up.

"Well," said Grandma. "Well. How about that?"

The coyote sat down, looking pleased with itself, which is the natural state of coyotes.

Marguerite's skin and eyes were brown, no longer gray and white. She reached into her mouth and pried the silver cuff out of her tongue. Her young companion, no longer feathered, spat blood. He was older than Grandma had thought. It was his wounded eyes that made him look so young.

His name was John, Marguerite told her. (Privately Grandma suspected that was nothing like his name, but she wouldn't have given her real name to the cold-king either.) He had been captured not long after Marguerite. His people were to the south and east. "I'll see him home," she said, looking at Grandma, as if she expected her to argue.

It did not matter in the least to Grandma, so long as she didn't have to deal with it. "Go into town and talk to Tomas," suggested Grandma. "Tell him I sent you. He'll loan you a mule."

They nodded together and stood, leaning against each other, the only two people in the desert who knew what it was like to be tongue-cut birds.

John spoke to Marguerite, and she translated. "Is the old man gone?"

"Don't know," said Grandma. "Things like that don't die easy. But I've never heard of anything coming back alive from inside a coyote."

The coyote looked, if possible, even more pleased. "My stomach is very dreadful," it said. "I eat carrion and dung, when I can get it."

"I don't think it'll be back for awhile, at least," said Grandma. "And if it is, you and John will know how to defeat him. You'll need a different third, though. I'm too old for this."

"Thank you," said Marguerite, and "Thank you," said John, pronouncing the words slowly and carefully.

"Weren't nothing," said Grandma, which was a lie and a half.

After they were gone, Grandma fell backward and just breathed for awhile. The shadows were growing very long. A whole day could not have passed in the ruins of the used-up people, but perhaps time had folded a little oddly too.

She heard the tracks sing, as if there was a train somewhere nearby, but it did not pass this way after all. That was just as well. She did not think she could deal with a god just now.

"Are you dead?" asked the coyote with interest.

"Don't get your hopes up," snapped Grandma. "I ain't dying just yet," and that may or may not have been a lie. She wasn't quite sure.

"Then you had better get up," said the coyote. "And I will walk a little way home with you, just in case you die along the way."

It took her a long time going home. The coyote walked her nearly all the way, keeping up a string of nonsense, and since she refused to show weakness in front of a coyote, she walked faster than she might have otherwise.

She refilled her water bottle at the last wash, and drank deeply. When she lowered the bottle, the coyote was gone.

"All right, then," she said. Not being grateful, because you never show gratitude to a coyote. But not being ungrateful, either. Just in case.

She walked until she saw the fence around her garden, and then she stood and looked and thought that perhaps she hadn't lied to the coyote about dying after all.

She went the last little way and opened the gate.

The cholla-bone girl sat on the back steps, carefully petting Spook-cat. She looked up at Grandma, her face very serious.

"My great-grandmother sent me," she said.

"I know," said Grandma wearily. She leaned against the gate-post.

"She says you're supposed to teach me," said the girl.

Grandma was silent. Wondering what an old jackalope wife could teach to a girl with bones made of cholla ribs. Wondering if there was anything she knew worth learning, after all.

She thought of the lessons in the desert, and thought that this girl probably knew them all already. They would have been written on the inside of her skin since the day before she was born.

Still, there was one thing she had worth passing on.

"Come on," said Grandma, pushing herself away from the fence. "We'll clean out the back room for you. But first, I'll teach you how to make a really good tomato sandwich."

# IN QUESTIONABLE TASTE

People ask if gardening is hard
but that's not the problem
the problem is it's easy
and it really ought to be impossible.

What is this
putting stuff in dirt and expecting to get food back
what are you, a communist?
You bought a bag of cowpeas
not even a proper seed packet with a glossy picture on it
and shoved a couple in the ground.
You know it can't work.

Even fairy tales know better
everybody laughs when Jack trades a cow for beans
a cow is worth something, after all.
The whips that twined up into the hydrangeas have three green leaves
so they must be poison ivy
that's probably it
the things that look like bean pods are a coincidence
it's a new kind of poison ivy
you'll probably be even more allergic to this one.

And the funny thing is that I know this
when they come for me and say "You have to stop now—
you know people aren't allowed to do this sort of thing,"

# IN QUESTIONABLE TASTE

I'll bow my head and say "I know."
It was much too easy
it had to be illegal
or at least in very questionable taste,
thinking you could put almost nothing into dirt
and get everything back
almost for free.

# ORIGIN STORY

*My friend Jared wrote synopses for several fake fairy tales. It was a joke, but I wanted to read some of those stories, and what with one thing and another…*

The last of the fairies worked in a charnel house, taking apart the beasts that came dead under her hands. In her youth, she had been the last and least of three; now she was the only living one, and even fairies must earn their keep.

At night, when the knackermen went home, she made creatures out of meat and bone and scraps of skin. It was an act of creation to balance out the destruction in her days. When she had stuffed the little puppets full, she licked her fingers and wrote their names on the outside of the casing in blood and spittle.

The smallest ones would come alive immediately and toddle out through the massive doors. Eyeless, they looked around at the city before them; lungless, they squeaked and squalled their delight; mindless, they scurried into the shadows, to spread malice and alarm.

I never said she was a *good* fairy, you know.

The first of her charnel children were small and held together mostly with magic. But, as she learned the way that animals fit together, the way sinew embraces bone and organs entwine under ribs, they grew more complex. She sewed them together with needle and thread, murmuring to herself. They took longer to wake up, and they lasted longer once they did.

She spent months making birds or bats or something in between the two. The slaughterhouse did not do birds, but she found a winter-killed crow and studied how it fitted together, the delicate keelbone and the folded wrists of wings. (She had little interest in feathers, but scraped sausage casings made excellent wing membranes and were more easily sewn up.)

The first dozen or so were flightless. Not by design, but from ignorance. They tried to fly and fell to earth, where they rolled and flopped like rabid bats, and the fairy grumbled because she knew that she had not quite got it right.

One morning, in the gray light before dawn, she launched one out the door and it spread its wings and flew.

It had no head—heads were, to the fairy's way of thinking, largely superfluous—but it had immense wings and it flapped them like a goose. It soared across the city and was caught by the wind. She saw it rolling in midair, struggling to steer, and then it was swept away out of sight.

The fairy smiled in the shadow of the great killing chute.

The next bird she built had a tail studded with sow's ears for a rudder. It churned the air like a slave galley, wallowing on the wind, but it rose and fell and corrected itself and rose again.

She built many more after that, and came back to them whenever she was feeling particularly cross. The people in the poor part of the city began to whisper of things that crawled across the thin roofs, making wet, rubbery sounds, of piles of offal found in the gutter that not even the dogs would touch.

When she had mastered the art of flight, the fairy began to branch out. She made river swimmers and great undulating serpents and many-legged things that scurried on feet of pointed bone.

She made human-like ones too, of course. Fairies find that sort of thing amusing. She made charnel children that walked on two legs and she put pig tongues in their mouths to make them speak.

In the poor part of the city, they began to talk of things that passed the doors in the night, calling nonsense to each other in papery voices.

Yes, she did once make a beautiful one. Do you think I don't know how to tell a story? She made one with translucent skin and the eyes of a stillborn calf, and she taught it to sing and to sigh.

But this is not that creature's story.

Eventually, the slaughterhouse workers figured out that something strange was going on. It took longer than it might have, because the fairy's glamour could still haze mortal minds, but they began to notice that more scraps were going missing than could be explained by simple theft. And it occurred to some of them, slowly, that she was always there, that she did not seem to go home at night. At first they might have thought that she had no home to go to, which had no shame in it, but gradually they learned differently.

Nevertheless, the fairy was allowed to continue. She was an enormously skilled worker, and if you believe that butchery is unskilled labor, you have never tried it for yourself. And to give her credit where it is due, when she worked, the beasts walked calm to their deaths instead of fighting. When the ancient horses came to be knackered, she stood beside them and then they did not fear the smell of blood, and they died tired but easy, and went on to whatever waits for old horses on the other side.

Goats respected her. Goats respect very little, but they recognized some of themselves in her, and so they gave her what courtesy goats give to each other. (This is hardly any, of course, but a trifle more than none at all.) The Judas goat that worked in the slaughterhouse considered her a colleague instead of a necessary annoyance.

The human workers may not have wanted to consider her a colleague, but between fear and respect, they grew used to it. Jobs were not so plentiful that many could afford to lose theirs. And everyone knew, of course, that the owner would side with the fairy...the owner, and his strange mistress with translucent skin and huge calf eyes, who could only sing and sigh.

A few seasons after the fairy mastered birds, a spotted mare came to the slaughterhouse.

She was a draft horse mare and her legs were feathered with long white silk. She had hooves as large as dinner plates and a coat like the night sky in reverse—white dappled with flecks of black. Her neck was arched and there were marks on her coat where a harness had worn against her skin.

The fairy rarely spoke aloud, but she looked into the mare's face and said, "This one should not be here."

The foreman looked up, startled. He would have taken that from no other worker, but he respected both the fairy and the Judas goat, as creatures who were not like him, but did their jobs and did them well.

"She is past foaling," said the foreman, "and hay and grain is very dear. The owner cannot feed her and cannot sell her. So he says."

The fairy reached up her thin gray hands and caressed the draft mare's cheek.

The mare looked into the fairy's eyes and turned her head a little to lip at the gray fingers. She knew perfectly well where she was and the fate that awaited her. If the fairy had to guess, she would have said that the mare was bleakly amused.

Until then, she had not known that horses were capable of such complexity. The mare's eyes were an education.

"They mean to kill you," said the fairy quietly.

The mare knew. The mare had served men faithfully and well, hauling loads and bearing foals, and now they had failed to hold their end of the bargain. She would have rather been tied to a great load and hauled it until her heart burst, that she might die in the traces, but it had not been given to her to choose.

The foreman waited. He kept his eyes on the floor, respectfully, as if he were in church. He knew that what was passing between the mare and his best butcher was not a canny thing, and he knew also that he would not speak of it to anyone.

(He was wrong, incidentally. Many years later, as he lay dying, he would tell the priest at his bedside. "Was it a sin?" he asked, when he had finished. "Should I have stopped her?"

The priest was old and he had seen things that they had not taught him in seminary, and he said, "Some things, I think, have nothing to do with sin. They are simply none of our business."

The foreman was comforted, and he laid back in his bed and died not long after. But this is not his story either.)

The fairy stood by the mare's head while the knackers came, and the men with hammers. She was close enough to hear the mare's last thought—"Ah, well,"—and the strength and bemusement and resignation in that thought woke a rage in the fairy's chest that she had not felt since her sisters had died.

When the bloody work was done, she drove the other butchers away and set to work herself.

A man named Throat, who had worked at the slaughterhouse for only a few weeks, tried to argue. He went and found the foreman and brought him back so that he could see the fairy, hunched over the hide and the hooves and the heart, like a great gray rat.

"She'd not doing what she's s'posed to," said Throat.

The fairy lifted her head and looked into the foreman's eyes.

Perhaps the glamour slipped just a little, or perhaps the foreman had already seen too much. He turned to Throat and shouted that when he was the best worker in the slaughterhouse, he could damn well do what he pleased, but until that time, he'd keep his eyes on his own business and his tongue behind his teeth.

The foreman was not given to shouting, and he regretted it later. But as I said, this is not his story.

"I will make something great of you," whispered the fairy to the horse's bones. "I will make something that no one has ever seen before." And her knives flashed in the dim light and blood spread over the pale white hide and stained it the color of a city sky at night.

She did no more work on the line that night and no one questioned her. The men—and yes, a few women—who worked in the slaughterhouse closed up the doors and shut the gates, sluiced the floors and cleaned their tools. The foreman was the last man out, and he turned off the oil lamps and closed the door, leaving the fairy in the darkness.

She did not mind. She could see by heat and starlight. Her small knife moved as surely in the dark as in the light.

It did not stop moving even a few hours later, when Throat snuck back into the building.

He probably thought that he was being stealthy. His footfalls were muffled and he breathed silently though his mouth (although this is usually wise in a slaughterhouse, in any event). He waited for his eyes to adjust so that he did not blunder into anything in the dark.

But the building was very quiet and his footsteps were very loud to the fairy's ears. She waited until he was only a few paces away, and said, "Why have you come back?"

Throat halted. She could see the surface of his mind and her death was in it, waiting on the point of his axe.

"You're doing wicked work," said Throat. "It ain't canny. It ain't right."

"That is true," said the fairy, licking a bit of thread to stiffen it. She threaded it deftly through the needle, while Throat worked himself up to the point of killing.

"You shouldn't be doing it," said Throat. "It's devil-work."

The fairy laughed, and Throat flinched away from the sound. "Fairy," she said. "Not devil. We are not the same, though we recognize each other when we meet in the street —"

"You shouldn't be doing it!" said Throat again, louder.

"So stop me," said the fairy, her back turned to him.

It took him a moment more. His mouth worked and he wanted to have said, "I will!" right away, but he had waited too long and now it would seem stupid. The fairy loved how human that was, that he was about to try to kill her and he was still worried that he had spoken up too late.

"I'll stop you now!" he said, a little too loudly, as if that would make it seem like his idea, and then he leapt forward and swung the axe.

Glamour was far easier to work in the dark. She was three feet to the right of where he thought she was. The axe cleft the air with a whistling sound.

She caught his leg in one hand and flung him aside. Her right hand never slowed with the needle and thread. The back of Throat's head struck the floor and his legs shuddered and spasmed like a spider.

Even the least and weakest of fairies was a match for anything but iron.

The fairy tied off the thread neatly and rose to her feet. Throat was still alive, but the blow to his head would likely have killed him. The fairy finished the job, coolly, and laid him out next to the body of the spotted mare.

His brain was a warm gray bird, still alive and fluttering inside his skull. She plucked its wings and cast a few essential bits aside, leaving the rest for later…and that was the end of Throat's story.

The fairy had little use for him as a living being, but as a scaffold of bone to hang her creation on, he would be very useful indeed.

The fairy worked all night and most of the day. It was the holy day, when no one worked and the great doors remained closed, so the fairy was able to take her time. Light shone through the cracks in the doors, thin bars shining down on her and catching flecks of bone dust in the air.

Throat had been a large man, but not large enough for her purposes. She cracked his ribs open and threw his heart aside. Human hearts were small and complicated things. The mare's heart was large and purposeful. She rebuilt the lungs around it and closed it up in ribs cobbled together from horse and human bone.

Then came shoulders large enough to flank the ribs, and hips built out with draft horse muscle. The scaffold began to seem too short, so the fairy broke the creature's legs and splinted them up again, longer and stronger than before. Still human-shaped, but larger, a body fit to carry the weight of the horse's heart.

The fairy examined Throat's genitals and found them unnecessarily complicated. Female parts were far easier to replicate with knife and magic, and it was not as if the horse-hearted creature would need to reproduce itself.

Herself, now.

Nerves were delicate, troublesome work, and the fairy used magic to knit them together. Most of it, though, was needle and thread and sinew and bone, over and over, long enough even for a fairy's fingers to tire.

It was not so bad as spinning straw into gold, this spinning of cold meat into live flesh. Straw gouged and jabbed her fingertips, until she left bloody streaks across the piles of gold, and this was soft. But it was still cold, stiff work, and the fairy was not so young as she had been.

She rose at last, on the edge of twilight, to stretch and grimace. She had rebuilt her creature's face, wrapping the delicate mare's skin over Throat's skull. Some of his teeth had been bad, and a horse's molars would not go easily in a human mouth, so the fairy had picked up pig teeth from the floor and slipped them into her creature's gums.

Her back ached. This was a greater work than any she had ever made. Bringing it to life might kill her, or at least drink the better part of her magic dry, but she did not care. It was too important to finish her creation and see it live and keep the oath she had not quite sworn to the spotted mare.

She stood in the doorway and rubbed her back, watching the bats and the nighthawks swooping over the rooftops. And then—yes, one of her flying beasts, a little roly-poly one that always seemed on the edge of crashing but which always righted itself just in time, barreling through the air while the bats shrilled alarm around it.

She smiled and turned back to her creation.

Nearly done, now.

Now there was only skin and hair to braid up around the flesh. This, too, was delicate, troublesome work, but she had renewed energy now that she was close to finished.

She left the long white feathers at the back of the legs—how could she not?—and pulled the mane down the back of the creature's neck and spine. She had to stop often now and go to the water butt to wash her hands and sluice blood away from the speckled hide.

The second time she did this, the hide twitched, like a horse shivering to flick away a fly. The fairy nodded. Usually her creations came to life much sooner.

She had not, quite, begun to doubt, but relief fired her hands anyway, and made the work go swiftly.

And then, quite suddenly, it was done.

The fairy looked for things to do, things left undone, but there was nothing. The stitches were small and neat and exact. She snipped a single loose thread and then she licked her finger and wrote a word across the creature's forehead.

"Breathe," she commanded.

The creature lay silently for a long, long moment, and then she inhaled, deeper than a human could. Her chest rose and fell and the great mare's heart beat under her ribs, so loud at first that the fairy could hear it—*thud. thud. thud.*

"Up!" said the fairy, and the creature rolled to her feet.

There was a fraction of an instant when the working nearly failed. The femurs ground in their sockets, their heads like hammers against the bone. Horse and human marrow flowed together, held with twine and stitches and fairy magic, and almost—*almost*—could not hold.

*"Up,"* growled the fairy, feeling years of her life peeling away like blistered skin. A little less of eternity, a few decades less in the slaughterhouse. No matter.

The creature swayed a bit, then locked her legs and stood. Nearly seven feet tall, solid as stone, a great living beast with human mind and horse's heart.

Her chest rose and fell again, and something caught, like a fish-hook under the fairy's heart. And pulled and pulled and…held.

The mare-woman turned her head from side to side, looked down at the fairy, and then she dropped down to her knees.

The fairy inhaled sharply, afraid that something had gone wrong—was it the legs, had she left them too thin, had the bones not meshed as they were supposed to—and then the mare-woman bowed her head down to the fairy in obeisance that was half-equine and half-human.

"Up," said the fairy again, deeply pleased and even more deeply exhausted.

The mare-woman rose and towered over her.

From a distance, one would think the creature a large human. Close up, the differences would be more obvious, but that was not the fairy's problem. Once she set them loose, they found their own way.

"Go on, then," said the fairy. She wanted to sleep. Perhaps she would go to the room with the calf-eyed charnel bride and take a few hours rest on a real mattress. "Go on."

And when the mare-woman looked at her, puzzled, she shook her head and shooed her out like a housewife with a chicken. "Go on! Shoo!"

The mare-woman went.

When she stepped onto the wooden stairs, they creaked under her weight. The fairy watched her walk away, one powerful, deliberate step at a time.

She wished that she'd been able to make hooves work, but the balance was always a problem when your creatures walked upright.

"Go to the river," she called after the mare-woman. "Wash off the blood."

The mare-woman turned and dipped her head. She lifted her face, sniffed, and then strode off in the direction of the river.

The fairy's last sight of her was a shadow, monstrous and beautiful, spreading across the stones behind her.

The mare-woman walked through the streets in the dimness. Throat's memories, half-gone and half-useless, nevertheless included *city* and *river.* And *blood*, as a thing to be washed clean.

This is the beginning of her story, though the rest is not yet written.

As for the fairy, she leaned against the wall, exhausted. The power had gone out of her like blood flowing from the jugular, and she was more tired than she had been since her sisters died.

She had made a great thing. Whether it was good or evil or neither or both did not much matter. Heroes or monsters are equally impressive, in their own way.

*I will never make anything so great again,* she thought.

A human might have felt disappointed. The charnel fairy mostly felt relief.

She dozed a little and woke when her sleeve jabbed her. She had threaded the needle through it, to keep it out of the way. The tip was still sharp.

She stifled a yawn.

The sun was not yet up. And there were still a great many scraps leftover, and some of them were too obviously human. It would be inconvenient if anyone found them.

*Well...*

Humming to herself, she picked up what was left of Throat and began to piece together another leather bird.

# POCOSIN

*Pocosins are a type of raised peat wetland found almost exclusively in the Carolinas. The name derives from an Eastern Algonquian word meaning "swamp on a hill." They are a rare and unique ecosystem, today widely threatened by development. I am very fond of them.*

This is the place of the carnivores, the pool ringed with sundews and the fat funnels of the pitcher plants.

This is the place where the ground never dries out and the loblolly pines grow stunted, where the soil is poor and the plants turn to other means of feeding themselves.

This is the place where the hairstreak butterflies flow sleekly through the air and you can hear insect feet drumming inside the bowl of the pitcher plants.

This is the place where the old god came to die.

He came in the shape of the least of all creatures, a possum. Sometimes he was a man with a long rat's tail, and sometimes he was a possum with too-human hands. On two legs and four, staggering, with his hands full of mud, he came limping through the marsh and crawled up to the witchwoman's porch.

"Go back," she said, not looking up. She had a rocking chair on the porch and the runners creaked as she rocked. There was a second chair, but she did not offer it to him. "Go back where you came from."

The old god laid his head on the lowest step. When he breathed, it hissed through his long possum teeth and sounded like he was dying.

"I'm done with that sort of thing," she said, still not looking up. She was tying flies, a pleasantly tricky bit of work, binding thread and chicken feathers to the wickedness of the hook. "You go find some other woman with witchblood in her."

The old god shuddered and then he was mostly a man. He crawled up two steps and sagged onto the porch.

The woman sighed and set her work aside. "Don't try to tell me you're dying," she said grimly. "I won't believe it. Not from a possum."

Her name was Maggie Grey. She was not so very old, perhaps, but she had the kind of spirit that is born old and grows cynical. She looked down on the scruffy rat-tailed god with irritation and a growing sense of duty.

His throat rasped as he swallowed. He reached out a hand with long yellow nails and pawed at the boards on the porch.

"Shit," Maggie said finally, and went inside to get some water.

She poured it down his throat and most of it went down. He came a little bit more alive and looked at her with huge, dark eyes. His face was dirty pale, his hair iron gray.

She knew perfectly well what he was. Witchblood isn't the same as godblood, but they know each other when they meet in the street. The question was why a god had decided to die on her porch, and that was a lousy sort of question.

"You ain't been shot," she said. "There's not a hunter alive that could shoot the likes of you. What's got you dragging your sorry ass up on my porch, old god?"

The old god heaved himself farther up on the porch. He smelled rank. His fur was matted with urine when he was a possum and his pants were stained and crusted when he was a man.

His left leg was swollen at the knee, a fat bent sausage, and the foot beneath it was black. There were puncture wounds in his skin. Maggie grunted.

"Cottonmouth, was it?"

The old god nodded.

Maggie sat back down in the rocking chair and looked out over the sundew pool.

There was a dense mat of shrubs all around the house, fetterbush and sheep laurel bound up together with greenbrier. She kept the path open with an axe, when she bothered to keep it open at all. There was no one to see her and the dying man who wasn't quite a man.

Mosquitos whined in the throats of the pitcher plants and circled the possum god's head. Maggie could feel her shoulders starting to tense up. It was always her shoulders. On a bad day, they'd get so knotted that pain would shoot down her forearms in bright white lines.

"Would've preferred a deer," she said. "Or a bear, maybe. Got some dignity that way." Then she laughed. "Should've figured I'd get a possum. It'd be a nasty, stinking sort of god that wanted anything to do with me."

She picked up a pair of scissors from where she'd been tying flies. "Hold still. No, I ain't gonna cut you. I ain't so far gone to try and suck the poison out of a god."

It had likely been another god that poisoned him, she thought—Old Lady Cottonmouth, with her gums as white as wedding veils. She saw them sometimes, big, heavy-bodied snakes, gliding easy through the water. Hadn't ever seen the Old Lady, but she was out there, and it would be just like a possum to freeze up when those white gums came at him, sprouting up fangs.

Even a witch might hesitate at that.

She waited until he was a man, more or less, and cut his pant leg open with the scissors. The flesh underneath was angry red, scored with purple. He gasped in relief as the tight cloth fell away from the swollen flesh.

"Don't thank me," she said grimly. "Probably took a few hours off your life with that. But they wouldn't be anything worth hanging on for."

She brought him more water. The first frogs began to screek and squeal in the water.

"You sure you want this?" she asked. "I can put a knife across your throat, make it easy."

He shook his head.

"You know who's coming for you?"

He nodded. Then he was a possum again and he gaped his mouth open and hissed in pain.

She hesitated, still holding the scissors. "Ain't sure I want to deal with 'em myself," she muttered. "I'm done with all that. I came out here to get *away*, you hear me?"

The possum closed his eyes, and whispered the only word he'd ever speak.

"*...sorry...*"

Maggie thrust the scissors into her pocket and scowled.

"All right," she said. "Let's get you under the porch. You come to me and I'll stand them off for you, right enough, but you better not be in plain sight."

She had to carry him down the steps. His bad leg would take no weight and he fell against her, smelling rank. There were long stains on her clothes before they were done.

Under the porch, it was cool. The whole house was raised up, to save it from the spring floods, when the sundew pool reached out hungry arms. There was space enough, in the shadow under the stairs, for a dying god smaller than a man.

She didn't need to tell him to stay quiet.

She went into the house and poured herself a drink. The alcohol was sharp and raw on her throat. She went down the steps again, to a low green stand of mountain mint, and yanked up a half dozen stems.

They didn't gentle the alcohol, but at least it gave her something else to taste. The frogs got louder and the shadows under the sheep laurel got thick. Maggie sat back in her rocking chair with her shoulders knotting up under her shirt and went back to tying flies.

Someone cleared his throat.

She glanced up, and there was a man in preacher's clothes, with the white collar and clean black pants. The crease in them was pressed sharp enough to draw blood.

"Huh," she said. "Figured the other one'd beat you here."

He gave her a pained, fatherly smile.

She nodded to the other chair. "Have a seat. I've got bad whiskey, but if you cut it with mint and sugar, it ain't bad."

"No, thank you," said the preacher. He sat down on the edge of the chair. His skin was peat colored and there was no mud on his shoes. "You know why I've come, Margaret."

"Maggie," she said. "My mother's the only one who calls me Margaret, and she's dead, as you very well know."

The preacher tilted his head in acknowledgment.

He was waiting for her to say something, but it's the nature of witches to outwait God if they can, and the nature of God to forgive poor sinners their pride. Eventually he said "There's a poor lost soul under your porch, Maggie Grey."

"He didn't seem so lost," she said. "He walked here under his own power."

"All souls are lost without me," said the preacher.

Maggie rolled her eyes.

A whip-poor-will called, placing the notes end to end, whip-er-*will!* whip-er-*will!*

It was probably Maggie's imagination that she could hear the panting of the god under the porch, in time to the nightjar's calls.

The preacher sat, in perfect patience, with his wrists on his knees. The mosquitos that formed skittering sheets over the pond did not approach him.

"What's there for a possum in heaven, anyway?" asked Maggie. "You gonna fill up the corners with compost bins and rotten fruit?"

The preacher laughed. He had a gorgeous, church-organ laugh and Maggie's heart clenched like a fist in her chest at the sound. She told her heart to behave. Witchblood ought to know better than to hold out hope of heaven.

"I could," said the preacher. "Would you give him to me if I did?"

Maggie shook her head.

His voice dropped, a father explaining the world to a child. "What good does it do him, to be trapped in this world? What good does it do anyone?"

"He seems to like it."

"He is a prisoner of this place. Give him to me and I will set him free to glory."

"He's a possum," said Maggie tartly. "He ain't got much use for glory."

The preacher exhaled. It was most notable because, until then, he hadn't been breathing. "You cannot doubt my word, my child."

"I ain't doubting nothing," said Maggie. "It'd be just exactly as you said, I bet. But he came to me because that's not what he wanted, and I ain't taking that away from him."

The preacher sighed. It was a more-in-sorrow-than-in-anger sigh, and Maggie narrowed her eyes. Her heart went back to acting the way a witch's heart ought to act, which was generally to ache at every damn thing and carry on anyway. Her shoulders felt like she'd been hauling stones.

"I could change your mind," he offered.

"Ain't your way."

He sighed again.

"Should've sent one of the saints," said Maggie, taking pity on the Lord, or whatever little piece of Him was sitting on her porch. "Somebody who was alive once, anyway, and remembers what it was like."

He bowed his head. "I will forgive you," he said.

"I know you will," said Maggie kindly. "Now get gone before the other one shows up."

Her voice sounded as if she shooed the Lord off her porch every day, and when she looked up again, he was gone.

It got dark. The stars came out, one by one, and were reflected in the sundew pool. Fireflies jittered, but only a few. Fireflies like grass and open woods, and the dense mat of the swamp did not please them. Maggie lit a lamp to tie flies by.

The Devil came up through a stand of yellowroot, stepping up out of the ground like a man climbing a staircase. Maggie was pleased to see that he had split hooves. She would have been terrible disappointed if he'd been wearing shoes.

He kicked aside the sticks of yellowroot, tearing shreds off them, showing ochre-colored pith underneath. Maggie raised an eyebrow at this small destruction, but yellowroot is hard to kill.

"Maggie Gray," said the fellow they called the Old Gentleman.

She nodded to him, and he took it as invitation, dancing up the steps on clacking hooves. Maggie smiled a little as he came up the steps, for the Devil always was a good dancer.

He sat down in the same chair that the preacher had used, and scowled abruptly. "See I got here late."

"Looks that way," said Maggie Gray.

He dug his shoulderblades into the back of the chair, first one then the other, rolling a little, like a cat marking territory in something foul. Maggie stifled a sigh. It had been a good rocking chair, but it probably wasn't wise to keep a chair around that the Devil had claimed.

"You've got something I want, Maggie Gray," he said.

"If it's my soul, you'll be waiting awhile," said Maggie, holding up a bit of feather. She looped three black threads around it, splitting the feather so it looked like wings. The hook gleamed between her fingers.

"Oh no," said the Devil, "I know better than to mess with a witch's soul, Maggie Gray. One of my devils showed up to tempt your great-grandmother, and she bit him in half and threw his horns down the well."

Maggie sniffed. "Well's gone dry," she said, trying not to look pleased. She knew better than to respond to demonic flattery. "It's the ground hereabouts. Sand and moss and swamps on top of hills. Had to dig another one, and lord knows how long it'll last."

"Didn't come here to discuss well-digging, Maggie Grey."

"I suppose not." She bit off a thread.

"There's an old god dying under your porch, Maggie Grey. The fellow upstairs wants him, and I aim to take him instead."

She sighed. A firefly wandered into a pitcher plant and stayed, pulsing green through the thin flesh. "What do you lot want with a scrawny old possum god, anyway?"

The Devil propped his chin on his hand. He was handsome, of course. It would have offended his notion of his own craftsmanship to be anything less. "Me? Not much. The fellow upstairs wants him because he's a stray bit from back before he and I were feuding. An old loose end, if you follow me."

Maggie snorted. "Loose end? The possum gods and the deer and Old Lady Cottonmouth were here before anybody thought to worship you. Either of you."

The Devil smiled. "Can't imagine there's many worshippers left for an old possum god, either. 'Cept the possums, and they don't go to church much."

Maggie bent her head over the wisp of thread and metal. "He doesn't feel like leaving."

Her guest sat up a little straighter. "I am not sure," he said, silky-voiced, "that he is strong enough to stop me."

Maggie picked up the pliers and bent the hook, just a little, working the feathers onto it. "He dies all the time," she said calmly. "You never picked him up the other times."

"Can only die so many times, Maggie Grey. Starts to take it out of you. Starts to make you tired, right down to the center of your bones. You know what that's like, don't you?"

She did not respond, because the worst thing you can do is let the Devil know when he's struck home.

"He's weak now and dying slow. Easy pickings."

"Seems like I might object," she said quietly.

The Devil stood up. He was very tall and he threw a shadow clear over the pool when he stood. The sundews folded their sticky leaves in where the shadow touched them. Under the porch steps, the dying god moaned.

He placed a hand on the back of her chair and leaned over her.

"We can make this easy, Maggie Gray," he said. "Or we can make it very hard."

She nodded slowly, gazing over the sundew pool.

"Come on—" the Devil began, and Maggie moved like Old Lady Cottonmouth and slammed the fish-hook over her shoulder and into the hand on the back of her chair.

The Devil let out a yelp like a kicked dog and staggered backwards.

"You come to *my* house," snapped Maggie, thrusting the pliers at him, "and you have the nerve to threaten me? A witch in her own home? I'll shoe your hooves in holy iron and throw *you* down the well, you hear me?"

"Holy iron won't be kind to witchblood," he gasped, doubled over.

"It'll be a lot less kind to *you,*" she growled.

The Devil looked at his hand, with the fish-hook buried in the meat of his palm, and gave a short, breathless laugh. "Oh, Maggie Gray," he said, straightening up. "You aren't the woman your great-grandmother was, but you're not far off."

"Get gone," said Maggie. "Get gone and don't come back unless I call."

"You will eventually," he said.

"Maybe so. But not today."

He gave her a little salute, with the hook still stuck in his hand, and limped off the porch. The yellowroot rustled as he sank into the dirt again.

His blood left black spots on the earth. She picked up the lantern and went to peer at the possum god.

He was still alive, though almost all possum now. His whiskers lay limp and stained with yellow. There was white all around his eyes and a black crust of blood over his hind leg.

"Not much longer," she said. "Only one more to go, and then it's over. And we'll both be glad."

He nodded, closing his eyes.

On the way back onto the porch, she kicked at a black bloodstain, which had sprouted a little green rosette of leaves. A white flower coiled out of the leaves and turned its face to the moon.

"Bindweed," she muttered. "Lovely. One more damn chore tomorrow."

She stomped back onto the porch and poured another finger of whiskey.

It was almost midnight when the wind slowed, and the singing frogs fell silent, one by one.

Maggie looked over, and Death was sitting in the rocking chair.

"Grandmother," she said. "I figured you'd come."

"Always," said Death.

"If you'd come a little sooner, would've saved me some trouble."

Death laughed. She was a short, round woman with hair as gray as Maggie's own. "Seems to me you were equal to it."

Maggie grunted. "Whiskey?"

"Thank you."

They sat together on the porch, drinking. Death's rocker squeaked in time to the breathing of the dying god.

"I hate this," said Maggie, to no one in particular. "I'm tired, you hear me? I'm tired of all these fights. I'm tired of taking care of things, over and over, and having to do it again the next day." She glared over the top of her whiskey. "And don't tell me that it *does* make a difference, because I know that, too. Ain't I a witch?"

Death smiled. "Wouldn't dream of it," she said.

Maggie snorted.

After a minute, she said "I'm so damn tired of *stupid.*"

Death laughed out loud, a clear sound that rang over the water. "Aren't we all?" she said. "Gods and devils, aren't we all?"

The frogs had stopped. So had the crickets. One whippoorwill sang uncertainly, off on the other side of the pond. It was quiet and peaceful and it would have been a lovely night, if the smell of the dying possum hadn't come creeping up from under the porch.

Death gazed into her mug, where the wilting mint was losing the fight against the whiskey. "Can't fix stupid," she said. "But other things, maybe. You feeling like dying?"

Maggie sighed. It wasn't a temptation, even with her shoulders sending bright sparks of pain toward her fingers and making the pliers hard to hold steady. "Feeling like resting," she said. "For a couple of months, at least. That's all I want. Just a little bit of time to sit here and tie flies and drink whiskey and let somebody else fight the hard fights."

Death nodded. "So take it," she said. "Nobody's gonna give it to you."

Maggie scowled. "I was," she said bitterly. "'Til a possum god showed up to die."

Death laughed. "It's why he came, you know," she said. Her eyes twinkled, just like Maggie's grandmother's had, when she wore the body that Death was wearing now. "He wanted to be left alone to die, so he found a witch that'd understand."

Maggie raked her fingers through her hair. "Son of a bitch," she said, to no one in particular.

Death finished her drink and set it aside. "Shall we do what's needful?"

Maggie slugged down the rest of the mug and gasped as the whiskey burned down her throat. "Needful," she said thickly. "That's being a witch for you."

"No," said Death, "that's being alive. Being a witch just means the things as need doing are bigger."

They went down the stairs. The boards creaked under Maggie's feet, but not under Death's, even though Death had heavy boots on.

Maggie crouched down and said "She's here for you, hon."

She would have sworn that the possum had no strength left in him, but he crawled out from under the porch, hand over hand. His hind legs dragged and his tail looked like a dead worm.

There was nothing noble about him. He stank and black fluid leaked from his ears and the corners of his eyes. Even now, Maggie could hardly believe that God and the Devil would both show up to bargain for such a creature's soul.

Death knelt down, heedless of the smell and the damp, and held out her arms.

The possum god crawled the last little way and fell into her embrace.

"There you are," said Death, laying her cheek on the spikey-furred forehead. "There you are. I've got you."

The god closed his eyes. His breath went out on a long, long sigh, and he did not draw another one.

Maggie walked away, to the edge of the sundew pool, and waited.

A frog started up, then another one. The water rippled as their throat sacs swelled. Something splashed out in the dark.

"It's done," called Death, and Maggie turned back.

The god look smaller now. Death had gathered him up and he almost fit in her lap, like a small child or a large dog.

"Don't suppose he's faking it?" asked Maggie hopefully. "They're famous for it, after all."

Death shook her head. "Even possum gods got to die sometime. Help me get him into the pond."

Maggie took him under the arms and Death took the feet. His tail dragged on the ground as they hauled him. Death went into the water first, sure-footed, and Maggie followed, feeling water come in over the tops of her shoes.

"If I'd been thinking, I would've worn waders," she said.

Death laughed Maggie's grandmother's laugh.

The bottom of the sundew pool was made of mud and sphagnum moss, and it wasn't always sure if it wanted to be solid or not. Every step she took required a pause while the mud settled and sometimes her heels sank in deep. She started to worry that she was going to lose her shoes in the pool, and god, wouldn't that be a bitch on top of everything else?

At least the god floated. Her shoulders weren't up to much more than that.

In the middle of the pool, Death stopped. She let go of the possum's feet and came around to Maggie's side. "This ought to do it," she said.

"If we leave the body in here, it'll stink up the pool something fierce," said Maggie. "There's things that come and drink here."

"Won't be a problem," Death promised. She paused. "Thought you were tired of taking care of things?"

"I am," snapped Maggie. "*Tired* isn't the same as *can't*. Though if this keeps up..."

She trailed off because she truly did not know what lay at the end of being tired and it was starting to scare her a little.

Death took the possum's head between her hands. Maggie put a hand in the center of his chest.

They pushed him under the water and held him for the space of a dozen heartbeats, then brought him to the surface.

"Again," said Death.

They dunked him again.

"Three times the charm," said Death, and they pushed him under the final time.

The body seemed to melt away under Maggie's hands. One moment it was a solid, hairy weight, then it wasn't. For a moment she thought it was sinking and her heart sank with it, because fishing a dead god out of the pond was going to be a bitch of a way to spend an hour.

But he did not sink. Instead he simply unmade himself, skin from flesh and flesh from bone, unraveling like one of her flies coming untied, and there was nothing left but a shadow on the surface of the water.

Maggie let out a breath and scrubbed her hands together. They felt oily.

She was freezing and her boots were full of water and something slimy wiggled past her shin. She sighed. It seemed, as it had for a long time, that witchcraft—or whatever this was—was all mud and death and need.

She was so damn tired.

She thought perhaps she'd cry, and then she thought that wouldn't much help, so she didn't.

Death reached out and took her granddaughter's hand.

"Look," said Death quietly.

Around the pond, the fat trumpets of the pitcher plants began to glow from inside, as if they had swallowed a thousand fireflies. The light cast green shadows across the surface of the water and turned the sundews into strings of cut glass beads. It cut itself along the leaves of the staggerbush and threaded between the fly-traps' teeth.

Whatever was left of the possum god glowed like foxfire.

Hand in hand, they came ashore by pitcher plant light.

Death stood at the foot of the steps. Maggie went up them, holding the railing, moving slow.

There were black stains on the steps where the god had oozed. She was going to have to scrub them down, pour bleach on them, maybe even strip the wood. The bindweed, that nasty little plant they called "Devil's Guts" was already several feet long and headed toward the mint patch. The stink of dying possum was coming up from under the steps and that was going to need to be scraped down with a shovel and then powdered with lime.

At least she could wait until tomorrow to take an axe to the Devil's rocking chair, though it might be sensible to drag it off the porch first.

The notion of all the work to be done made her head throb and her shoulders climb toward her ears.

"Go to bed, granddaughter," said Death kindly. "Take your rest. The world can go on without you for a little while."

"Work to be done," Maggie muttered. She held onto the railing to stop from swaying.

"Yes," said Death, "but not by you. Not tonight. I will make you this little bargain, granddaughter, in recognition of a kindness. I will give you a little time. Go to sleep. Things left undone will be no worse for it."

Death makes bargains rarely, and unlike the Devil, hers are not negotiable. Maggie nodded and went inside.

She fell straight down on the bed and was asleep without taking off her boots. She did not say goodbye to the being that wore her grandmother's face, but in the morning, a quilt had been pulled up over her shoulder.

The next evening, as the sun set, Maggie sat in her rocking chair and tied flies. Her shoulders were slowly, slowly easing. The pliers only shook a little in her hand.

She had dumped bleach over the steps, and the smell from under the porch had gone of its own accord. The bindweed…well, the black husks had definitely been bindweed, but something had trod upon it and turned it into ash. It was a kindness she hadn't expected.

Her whiskey bottle was also full, with something rather better than moonshine, although she suspected that a certain cloven-hooved gentleman might have been responsible for that.

The space on the porch where the other rocking chair had been ached like a sore tooth and caught her eye whenever she glanced over. She sighed. Still, the wood would keep the fire going for a couple of days, when winter came.

The throats of the pitcher plants still glowed, just a little. Easy enough to blame on tired eyes. Maggie wrapped thread around the puff of feather and the shining metal hook, and watched the glow from the corner of her eyes.

A young possum trundled out of the thicket, and Maggie looked up.

"Don't start," she said warningly. "I'll get the broom."

The possum sat down on the edge of the pond. It was an awkward, ungainly little creature, with big dark eyes and wicked kinked whiskers. It was halfway hideous and halfway sweet, which gave it something in common with witches.

Slowly, slowly, the moon rose and the green light died away. The frogs chanted together in the dark.

The possum stood up, stretched, and nodded once to Maggie Gray. Then it shuffled into the undergrowth, its long rat-tail held behind it.

*I will give you a little time*, Death had said.

She wondered what Death considered 'a little time.' An hour? A day? A week?

"A few weeks," she said, to the pond and the absent possum. "A few weeks would be good. A little time for myself. The world can get on just fine without me for a couple of weeks."

She wasn't expecting an answer. The whippoorwills called to each other over the pond, and maybe that was answer enough.

Maggie poured two fingers of the Devil's whiskey, with hands that did not shake, and raised the glass in a toast to the absent world.

# IT WAS A DAY

*Tor payed me money for this poem once. I always wanted to be published by Tor, I just didn't expect it to be for something with a line about phone-sex with Pierson's puppeteers. Still, that, too, was a day.*

It was a day a little bit like today
the way the clouds threw shadows over the hill
the day you realized that you weren't going to find your future.

You were never going to go to Mars
or Pern
or Krynn
You were never going to open the door that led, inexorably, to Narnia
(or even Telmar, you weren't picky, and you were confident of your ability
to lead the revolution.)

Inigo Montoya was not going to slap you on the back
and invite you to take up the mantle of the Dread Pirate Roberts.
There would be no sardonic Vulcans or Andorians;
you would never be handed an elegant weapon for a more civilized age.

That was a strange day.

It ranked up there with the day that you realized that everybody else saw the you in the mirror, not the you inside your head. Not the you that was lean and tough and clever, not the you with perfect hair and a resonant voice that never said "Um….?"

Not *that* you.

No, they got the one that was fat and wobbly and stiff inside with terror, the one who was a little scared of eye makeup, the one who wore black because it was better to be freaky than pathetic.

You were never terribly fond of *that* you.

It was a day not at all like today
a day where the sun shone very brightly around the edges
that you realized that you could write that future.

You could blot out all those old arguments in your head by asking each character "What happens next?"
"And what do you say?"
"And are there ninjas?"

It wasn't the old future, but it was close.
(Besides, by that point, you'd realized that Inigo probably bathed once a month and that when people stuck you with swords, you'd fall down and shriek, and also that your feet hurt. And writers get indoor plumbing
and birth control pills if they can get them.)

It was a rather odd day
though not entirely unexpected
when you met the people who were angry with you.

It took awhile to figure out. Much more than a day, in fact.

Eventually, it came to you that those people had a future, too,
but they hadn't quite realized they weren't going to find it
and they blamed you for the fact it wasn't here.

You were not the sort of person that lived in their future.
You were still too fat and too wobbly and much too weird, and you laughed too loudly
like a good-natured hyena
and you were not supportive of their high and lonely destiny.

And if you were here and their future wasn't
it was probably your fault
and if you went away
maybe they'd get to go to Mars after all
pal around with Tars Tarkas
have phone-sex with the Pierson's Puppeteers.

They got very mad about it.
You pictured them hopping,
arms and legs going up and down
like angry puppets
when somebody pulled the string coming out of their crotch.

It was all very strange.

It was a day sort of like last Tuesday
or maybe the Friday before last
when somebody came up
with a copy of your book
it was dog-eared and they looked like they might cry
and they said "Thank you."

It was a day.

# ACKNOWLEDGMENTS

This is for all the editors who bought some of these stories, the readers who enjoyed them, and the dogs who laid at my feet and produced extraordinary smells while I was writing them.

Most particularly, however, I must mention my dear friend Mur Lafferty. The year "Jackalope Wives" was winning awards, there were some rather dramatic political upheavals and infighting surrounding the Hugo Awards. The end result was that George R. R. Martin gave out his own awards, called "The Alfies" to the stories who would have been first on the short list of nominations if not for shenanigans. "Jackalope Wives" was one of these.

From my friend Mur's perspective, however, she was attending the post-Hugo party thrown by Mr. Martin when people in the next room began shouting for her. She entered an enormous ballroom to find Mr. Martin up on a balcony, waving an award she'd never heard of, and a huge crowd demanding a speech she hadn't written. She said the trip up the stairs to the balcony was like a nightmare where she forgot what classes she had and whether she was wearing pants, until someone explained that she was accepting on my behalf, whereupon she was thrilled (except for a vague, persistent fear that "The Rains of Castamere" would start playing and everyone in the hall would be horribly slaughtered, because it *was* George R. R. Martin's party.)

From my perspective, I woke up hungover after toasting all my friends who did win awards, drove to Waffle House for hangover hashbrowns, and then Mur began texting me this story and sending photos of my Alfie, being held by many of my dear friends in the science fiction community. I am not ashamed to admit that I broke down crying. Yes, at Waffle House. These things happen.

I treasure my Alfie, but I treasure Mur's friendship far more.

T. Kingfisher
Pittsboro, NC
April 2017

# ABOUT THE AUTHOR

T. Kingfisher is a pen-name for the Hugo-Award winning author and illustrator Ursula Vernon.

Ms. Kingfisher lives in North Carolina with her husband, garden, and disobedient pets. Using Scrivener only for e-books, she chisels the bulk of her drafts into the walls of North Carolina's ancient & plentiful ziggurats. She is fond of wombats and sushi, but not in the same way.

You can find links to all these books, new releases, artwork, rambling blog posts, links to podcasts and more information about the author at

www.tkingfisher.com

## Also Available from Argyll Productions

The River: a hodgepodge of arcologies and platforms in a band around Ceres full of dreamers, utopians, corporatists—and transformed humans, from those with simple biomods to the exotic alien xenos and the totemics, remade with animal aspects. Gail Simmons, an itinerant salvor living aboard her ship Kismet, has docked everywhere totemics like her are welcome…and a few places they're not.

But when she's accused of stealing a databox from a mysterious wreck, Gail lands in the crosshairs of corporations, governments and anti-totemic terrorists. Finding the real thieves is the easy part. To get her life back, Gail will have to confront a past she's desperate not to face—and what's at stake may be more than just her future.

Kismet by Watts Martin, $17.95, ISBN 978-1-61450-339-2

For Kip, growing up in shadow of the human men-only Prince George's College of Sorcery has been nineteen years of frustration. Magic comes naturally to him, yet he's not allowed to study sorcery because he's a Calatian—one of a magically created race of animal people. But when a mysterious attack leaves the masters desperate for apprentices, they throw their doors open, giving Kip his chance.

As he fights to prove his worth to the human sorcerers, he encounters other oddities: a voice that speaks only to him, a book that makes people forget he's there, and one of the masters who will only speak to him through a raven. Greater than any of those mysteries or even whether the College's attacker will return to finish the job is the mystery of how Kip and his friends can prove that this place is where they belong…

CPSIA information can be obtained
at www.ICGtesting.com
Printed in the USA
BVHW062049210323
660850BV00013B/309